ALONE

Timeless tales of tears, triumph and turmoil

Hartlepool Writers Group
2024

Supported by Library @ The Hub

COPYRIGHT & DISCLAIMER

THE CONTRIBUTORS

Ange Dunn
Chris Robinson
Irene Styles
John Blackbird
Colin Dunn
Mikaella Lock
T.R. Moran
Quentin Cope
T.H.
Christine Turnbull
Robert Blackburn
A.J. Lot

: Publishing: Typesetting: Production :

: Mecurian Books:

THE HARTLEPOOL WRITERS GROUP (HWG)

'ALONE' is the latest, 2024 literary production from members of the Hartlepool Writers Group (HWG). With donations from members covering an eclectic mix of subject matter and style, we hope that you, the reader, will find time to read them all. In some places you will hopefully smile and in others you might well be in need of that second glass of wine!

The need to write and the need to explore our minds to take ourselves elsewhere on occasion is within us all. The HWG is a collection of individuals who have a need to write; a need some would perhaps describe as a passion. By getting together once a month, and guided by HWG Facilitator Denise Sparrowhawk, members of the group are able to share their ideas, exercise some basic writing techniques and most importantly seek critique of their work from other members.

As more and more processed entertainment and thought divergence advertising bombards our modern lives, it is often difficult to consider starting the writing process. The pressures of caring for a young family perhaps leave little time for embarking on laying down a measured number of words - words that would be the beginnings of that elusive novel which is supposed to rest within the soul of all of us. Being a member of a writing group, such as the HWG, provides support, encouragement and, most of all the confidence to grab any spare minute you can to get your thoughts down on paper.

So, we hope you will enjoy this latest varied anthology of work from the HWG; the heartfelt emotions, spirited actions and possibly amusing storylines that lay between its pages.

CONTENTS

The theme of this Anthology is 'Isolation' and contains depictions of subjects that may only be suitable for a mature audience. Each piece in this collection is a work of fiction.

Just a former academic with a shotgun and a dog named Shep! A family holiday retreat turned into a refuge; a place of *isolation*, a place of reflection perhaps? But what about the dark thoughts, the death of loved ones and the intervention of a stranger.

Will the murderous virus sweeping the country, be the end of it all for everyone? Or will hope overcome the fear of death itself? Amy thought so and now, after bringing him back from the edge, he must find her and repay a debt; a debt as precious as life itself. Shep approves ... and that is possibly all the encouragement he needs.

The title may be misleading. This short piece provides the reader with a window into the perplexing world of a far from average Elf ... an elf who is someone often *isolated* from the realities of what is really happening around him. Confusing his life events with those of Bilbo Baggins appears to be a natural process for our sometimes bemused and regularly frustrated protagonist.

Yes, you may well recall a face often to be seen skipping across film sets and on TV, promoting a well-known line of realistic-looking garden Gnomes. No one seems to understand that the average Elf can't afford a JCB, but what would he need one of those for anyway?

And.

Chris Robinson. Fiction: Page 25

This short piece provides a view of life, distant past, and explores the social aspects of family life in the middle part of the last century. This was a time when TV only offered three channels, a time before computers and mobile phones ... and of course the dreaded Internet.

Crowded in the 'living' room in front of the 'telly', still wondering how a moving picture was captured from the 'ether' by a few aluminium poles, everyone viewed the black and white images in isolation. This was the start of the microchip revolution and new technologies that would *isolate* us even more from family conversation, direct social interaction and the ability to pursue our own particular brand of excellence.

This piece may well bring back memories and a smile for some more mature readers.

The Humble Tale of Bernie Bear.
Robert Blackburn. Fantasy: Page 27

Bernie, throughout the time span of his complete existence, may have been many things to many people, but no life experience had ever affected him as much as his enforced period of *isolation*. From his very first journey from factory to shelf, he sought affection.

When the day came, he was chosen by Sarah to be lifted from his shelf, and he knew the wait had been worth it. However, Sarah fell ill one day, and a series of events meant that Bernie would be lost for a very long time; a time spent completely on his own ... until!

Fruit, Bacteria At A Pinch, But No Bears.
Chris Robinson. Humour: Page 44

How to describe the fruity world of a 'Fruit and Veg' actor? You know the kind! Modern TV ads seem to be packed with them; acrobatic blueberries, singing and dancing sunflowers, and the odd fruit salad express racing across the screen to ensure all deliveries were at their very freshest.

However, it can be a solitary existence for actors ... individuals who suffer most of it in *isolation*; a world where they spend their life being dressed as anything but themselves.

Yet who knows? It's possible the next gig might end up with our beloved (but unknown) actor even playing a bear? Well, approval or not, someone has to pay the bills!

Involuntary Isolation.
Irene Styles. Drama: Page 51

The clue is in the title with this short piece exposing the rawness of a post pandemic relationship between mother and daughter. What kind of cruelty would it be to strike down such a wonderful woman as her mother?

What enforced *isolation* was being brought to bear on a mind once so active, so enquiring ... and so full of mischief?

This wonderfully well written piece of flash fiction will make the reader ponder upon the fragilities of life and the relentless progress of us all toward a similar state of similar distress.

Last Words.
John Blackbird. Historical Fiction: Page 55

War at sea! Abandon ship! Possible survival! Inevitable *isolation*! This is the harrowing story of a young seaman; a story of his fight for survival after his ship sank beneath him in the dark waters of the North Sea during WWI. This was a war being fought at sea with the enemy looking to starve the island nation of Great Britain into a humiliating surrender.

It is a tale of courage and determination; a fight to live and a desire to battle once again another day!

Where will it end for this young, Able Seaman? Voices in the dark may spell a route to survival, or possibly an invitation to join his now dead comrades, slipping quietly away beneath the curling wave tops.

The minutes would seem like hours, and the voices would return ... but a decision might finally be made.

Red Card.
Colin Dunn. Short Story: Page 63

Simply a game of football! From the rush of adrenaline on the pitch to the *isolation* of a lonely, empty changing room.

The modern game of soccer will demand more than Ben is able to give.

Poor performance on the pitch, a marriage on the rocks and revenge on his mind will lead him to the front door of the betting shop ... and that's when the damage would really be done!

Right Up Scrooge's Street.
Chris Robinson. Mythology: Page 70

This very 'light' piece, from an author with a particular sense of humour, makes an uncommon connection between Scrooge, Jacob Marley, legendary Roman miser Iacobus Marlius and a stash of buried treasure.

With some characters seemingly *isolated* from reality, reference to 'Spookapedia' is sometimes required to keep this highly amusing piece moving at pace. But one thing is for sure ... once you've started, you will definitely have to finish!

Stew.
Mikaella Lock. Horror: Page 85

From the very start, this dark offering, beautifully written by a talented author, will have you hooked. The subject matter may well be controversial but the resilience and true grit character of the main actors is not. How will cruel, physical *isolation* and torture be managed?

Will escape from the clutches of a murdering madman be at all possible? Moving through several scenarios, the reader will be taken on a ride that starts and ends with a similar emotional explosion. Be prepared for a bumpy ride!

The Brown Paper Envelope.
Quentin Cope. Mystery: Page 132

Did Edward Pickering really know what was going on? Had he taken the precarious route of self-*isolation* to satisfy a personal misconnection, or simply insulate himself from the reality of having to raise two boisterous young children and a dog!

Christine, his wife of twenty years, was at the heart of it all.

He knew what was going on, or at least he felt quite sure he did, and that was what prompted him to write the damn email.

From that moment on, he had probably 'lost the game', and the reason why might well be found in the brown paper envelope. In hindsight, the decision to open it did not appear to have been a good one!

The Cave.
T.R. Moran. Fiction: Page 152

Perhaps Michael's guides should have known better. However, being left alone, *isolated* and unsure of what might happen next after a heavy rockfall, could not be blamed on them. Could he release himself from the dark labyrinth surrounding him without their help?

It might well be seen as unlikely. So, is there a foregone conclusion to this attention-grabbing piece? You will need to follow to the very end to find out!

The Nineteenth Day.
A.J. Lot. Fiction: Page 160

Sergeant Dominic Alvarez of Number 42 Commando was alive and kicking ... but only just. Had it simply been an *isolated* incident?

Someone had gone too far in a training regime that was arguably the toughest in the world.

Alvarez, however, was a patient man and once the opportunity for revenge raised its ugly head, he made a plan.

Ex Special Forces interrogator, Billie Dickson, was sure his holiday in Benidorm would provide him with many opportunities for cheap sex, some dedicated time roasting on the beach and the opportunity to sink copious quantities of beer.

So, what would happen when the two tough ex-soldiers came face to face once again? That would depend upon who ended up with their finger on the trigger! Whatever will be, will be as someone appears to have put themselves in line for a fall.

The Prisoner.
Ange Dunn. Fiction: Page 185

He had taken the life of a monster; the monster who brutally murdered his beautiful Maria. He was a prisoner now of course. The prison regime didn't scare him, the possible *isolation* did. This would not be physical isolation; no, if anything the prison estate was particularly overcrowded.

However, the mental and intellectual isolation might eventually wear him down. There could only be one refuge, and it had been chosen for him. He turned to page one and began to read!

The Target.
T.H. Drama: Page 193

A man at the top of his profession, he has honed his skills to perfection. But success has come at a price; he works in isolation. He has eschewed family and friends, such emotional ties would be a distraction and in his line of work distractions lead to mistakes, and mistakes could be catastrophic. Like every other job, his research for this one has been meticulous, his target is clear. All he has to do is wait for the right time and place to execute it – nothing can go wrong.

Trials & Tribulation.
Christine Turnbull. Fiction: Page 199

Alone in a life filled with the dreams of others; *isolated* from reality in the assignment of 'things not real' but needing to be dragged forth. This short piece explores a particular environment.

It observes its effects and emotions on a part of someone easily rebuffed by children not able to give themselves to understand and accept their ways. This powerful writing will doubtless leave a lasting impression on the reader.

Author Biographies.
Listing: Page 204

Aftermath
T.H.

Day 1 of my Journal.

I am embarking on this journal in the hope (perhaps forlorn) that someday, in future times, people will still be alive to read my experiences. I want to make one thing clear. I am not your typical survivalist with a grizzled beard reaching down to a jutting gut, a rack of high velocity firearms locked in my cupboard and a powerful beast of a motorbike chained up in a shed.

No, I'm just a former academic with a shotgun and a dog. I turned my back on the world, became a recluse. Our family's holiday retreat became my refuge.

When the third wave of the virus turned every home into a tomb and transformed the whole world into a mausoleum to lost humanity, I survived almost by chance and my chosen circumstance.

Sometimes, at night, I sit by my short-wave and turn the dials. Through the static I believe I can hear faint, phantom voices searching for human contact, and I remember that final call.

"Hello, Dad." Mel in close-up, pale face, smudges under her eyes.

"Can you see where I am?"

She adjusts the zoom. She is sitting on a park bench. Heavy blooms of lilac droop over her head.

It was my wife's favourite spot for a break after a heavy shift at the hospital.

"Mel, I see you in the open, in the middle of London. What on earth are you doing there?"

My sense of dread is filling my voice.

"I couldn't stay in the flat. Listen, Dad, please. Last night..." She hesitates, looks hard into the screen, begins again.

"Alice was coughing all night. This morning every movement, every effort to breath was agony; she wanted relief, you know, a final relief. She was choking, she couldn't … Oh Dad, I had to do it for her. I put the tube against her arm. She nodded; I pressed the plunger. She ... she whispered, "thank you"; she sort of smiled and ... her whole body just went limp."

"Mel, love, it was the only way for her. She knew that. Come up here. Join me."

"Lock down, Dad, no transport. Besides, it's too late."

"There's something I haven't told you."

I don't want to know. The words, 'Don't say this!' hammer in my brain.

She gazes into my face, "You've guessed, haven't you? So, it's a stroll in the sunshine, in the park, back to the flat and then ..."

She half-shrugs. "Oh, Dad, I'm so frightened."

She stretches her hand towards the screen: our fingers meet on that cold hard surface. The image freezes. The picture fades to grey. Time passes. I stare into the screen. Lost hours. My body shudders with dry sobs.

Day 2 of my Journal.

After breakfast, a sudden tense moment. Shep went into full alert: her hackles bristling, a low growl. She knows better than to draw unwanted attention by barking. A fox? In daylight? Not likely. Some other creature? A wild boar? Too quiet. Even a bold wolf. I had heard midnight howling. We waited, listening. Shep looked at me, expecting some response.

I placed the shotgun in the inner vestibule, unbarred and unlocked the outer door, swung the door open, my other hand on the gun. The path by the cottage was empty. I checked the rear area. Chicken run undamaged; the vegetable plot unplundered; the lean-to secure! So ... a false alarm perhaps? Only Shep looked disappointed at the lost chance of action.

Day 3 of my Journal.

This morning, I was out checking my snares when there was a shaking in nearby bushes, and surprise!

A figure appeared.

"Mister, you won't set your dog on me, will you?"

So this was my new neighbour, (but not for long, I hoped). Despite the mud-streaked face and ragged haircut beneath the bush hat, the voice was young and female.

"Just stay where you are!" in my most severe voice.

"It's O.K. Shep," to still the growl in her throat.

"Honest, I'm just passing through." Not true, she'd been around for a couple of days.

"On my way to friends in Newcastle."

Some hope of life there, I thought, but didn't say.

"Can you, can you spare me some food... please?" I considered, would it rid me of her or encourage her to stay?

"Right, I'll leave a parcel on my doorstep. Then I don't want you around."

"Anything you say," then an afterthought, "Thanks"

I watched her turn and trudge off into the woods. The food had gone from the step an hour later and, I hope, so had she.

Day 4 of my Journal.

The road surface was broken, buckled and potholed. Already saplings were thrusting through the cracks. The pathway was buried beneath an overgrowth of weeds and clumps of tall grasses. I was walking down the steep slope into Stanwell; behind me hillsides pitted by old limestone workings, below a pattern of grey slate roofs and square stone houses.

Once the scene would have been hidden by a heavy drift of chimney smoke, hanging over the large village which lay huddled by the curve in the river. In the main street the fronts of cottages are hidden behind rose-bushes grown wild, hedges stand tall as trees. I pass the play area: swings sway in the breeze, chains jingle, metal winces, waiting for the children who will never return.

A yellowing notice is still fixed to the chapel door.

'Prayer service for those who have gone

before. Remember your loved ones. 7.00 pm.'

The pub door stands ajar. In the half-light of morning the inside looks like an abandoned stageset: glasses still stand, some half-filled with amber liquid on the dust covered tables, a chair overturned, the shelves behind the bar empty, the smell of stale beer lingers in the air.

People just drank up, for one last time, said goodbye, went home, locked down, put the children to bed, and waited in hope, thinking we will be the ones who survive.

I stood on the bridge, watched the water swirl and foam. The fish weren't biting. The only thing I snagged was my hand on the hook: it tore a gash and drew blood. Careless and concerning. Back to Shep who had been left minding the house, just in case of intruders. Feel tired, am going to have an early night.

Day 5 of my Journal.

I can't remember much of the last few days or even how long I was ill. Vague moments of consciousness: waking to daylight, moments later it seemed, it was night - a shadowy figure. Panic. Someone was in the house. A cool hand on my forehead. A spoon held to my mouth. A female voice.

"Here, swallow this" I splutter. Mel! Mel is nursing me! I fight her off.

"Don't touch me. Keep away!" Am I protecting her from me or is this my coward's sense of self-preservation?

My body is shaking, soaked in sweat; I fall

back on the bunk. I was so sure it was Mel, just a figment of my delirium.

Then, this morning I woke to a heavy weight on my chest and Shep's muzzle in my face with a concerned look in her eyes. After a severe, overjoyed face-licking, I struggled on trembling legs to the table and, resting my body on it for support, I found a bowl of wildflowers and lodged beneath this note:

Heard your dog barking. Something was wrong. Sorry about the window. Thought I could help; you were kind to me. You were right out of it. Seem much better now. I'm pushing off. Know you don't want people around. I've taken some food. Stay well 'cos I won't be around to nurse you.
    Amy.

Was I really kind to you? Ah, Amy, you shame me.

Journal 3 days later.

Feeling much stronger. I have been thinking a lot, and I know what I must do. You could say I have had an epiphany. We must live together, or we will die alone. Today I am setting out to track down Amy. She can't have gone far. She is heading for a death zone: no city is yet safe. I owe her the chance of life - a life I can save.

She can return with me and live somewhere nearby if she wants to. Perhaps we can create a community of survivors, a pipe dream? Who knows? I am about to set off. Shep approves and is already waiting at the door. The house will be safe, locked and shuttered. I will give it just a few days and whatever my success or lack of it, I intend to return and complete my journal.

SOUTH DURHAM RECOVERY ZONE
The Stanwell Journal

This manuscript was discovered in an abandoned dwelling in Weardale. It is part of the Museum's small collection of documentary evidence from the period during and after the third pandemic. As such, it gives valuable insights into the way of life and the attitudes of one survivor.

THE END

An Average Elf
Chris Robinson

Yes, I'm an elf. Don't suppose you've seen an elf before; most people haven't. There's usually one or two of us about over here, this job or that ... it varies.

There is film consultancy, of course. Not that I'm asked to do that. You need connections, don't you? Like everything else. Same here with you, I suppose. No, what I do is make a bit of extra coming over here and modelling. Not making models, that is. No, I pose for them. One or two toy companies, mainly garden ornaments. Gnomes, you call them.

This firm's bringing out a new line, various activities; usual ones ... but new poses. I've been fishing in a birdbath, digging the vegetable patch, painting a big toadstool with a door in it and so on and so forth.

But I'm also using an electric thing to scrape the weeds out of the cracks between the paving stones in the drive. That is a first I gather. And, definitely without precedent, I'm flying a drone. It comes with a drone you can hang from a nearby fence or tree. They say that one should fly off the shelves.

Ever been to Elfland? You should go; you'll have a good holiday. Visitors are always welcome. Provided you don't mention Tolkien. Whatever you do, don't mention Tolkien. We're sick to death of Tolkien, Tolkien, Tolkien! Lord of the effing rings. It's a complete travesty of Elfland. No resemblance whatsoever. And of course, being an elf, what happens? I'm always getting asked,

"What epic adventures are you up to?"

Epic adventures!

"What monstrous entities are you going to slay this weekend?"

I feel like slaying somebody, no names no pack drill, and the monstrous entities can certainly wait for a millennium or two. I'm an average elf, with an average mortgage on an average elf-hole, and an average job in an average burrow.

What have I got to do with Bilbo Baggins? You never ask, do you? How does Bilbo Baggins have so much time on his hands?

You never ask the question you'd automatically ask if it were a human being. Oh, no, it's an elf, anything does for an elf.

Ask yourself now ... just ask yourself the obvious question. Did your wonderful Bilbo Baggins, your great Bilbo Baggins, this Bilbo Baggins you're so taken with, did this fabulous Bilbo Baggins ever have a real job? Of course not, no more than the rest. Private incomes the lot of them. We all know where the Baggins money comes from ... Joshua Charles Baggins, or rather Joshua Charles Baggins and sons, Bilbo being eighth out of nine.

Joshua Charles Baggins and Sons are millionaires the lot of them. Big in earthmoving equipment, Joshua Charles Baggins and Sons. I'm surprised you haven't heard of JCB.

I'll tell you what actually happened. Bilbo Baggins was sent to Oxford, don't you know. That's where Tolkien was, and who should interview him but you-know-who. As they do, I suppose, he asked him what he'd been doing recently.

Bilbo Baggins gave him the usual stuff; far-flung travels, epic adventures, taking the lead in helping others; like any rich kid in his gap year. Perhaps embroidered things a bit, par for the course.

And because it's an elf and anything goes for an elf, Tolkien writes it all down, doubtless with 'nobs' on, and the rest is history, which is precisely what it isn't so far as the average elf such as myself is concerned.

As I said, I've got an average mortgage on an average 'elfhole', and I've an 'elflet' on the way next month, and I need a new chamber in my 'elfhole' ... and I've got to dig it with my own bare hands. I can't afford a JCB. Not that you'd know that to read your Hobbit or your Lord of the Rings ... all three volumes. You show me where it says the average elf can't afford a JCB; you won't find it.

I tell them, I keep on telling them. They say, 'Oh, you're an elf, Bilbo Baggins, of course, Bilbo Baggins; you're just as I imagine him. Can you do the walk?'

I say 'look' and I tell them. Oh, yes ... I tell them alright. I say, 'Do you realise that the average elf can't afford a JCB?'

I look them in the eye, and I give it to them straight. They look at me as if I'm mad. It's not just any excavation; my 'elfhole' is next to a bog ... talking of which, excuse me while I go to the gents.

THE END

And
Chris Robinson

*(A solitary gentleman of a certain age reveals
exactly why he is solitary.)*

Now they're all 'Lucy in the Sky with iPhones'.
Different for us; we grew up without them, and we
can use them responsibly. When we were young, if
you wanted to talk to your friends while watching
television, you had to pick up a landline telephone
and you couldn't watch television while having a
Vesta curry followed by an Angel Delight.

Most families couldn't afford a television in the
kitchen, so you had to make the effort to go to the
kitchen, put them on a tray and carry them back
into the living room ... and you had to wait until
the adverts came on to do that.

However, you couldn't even do that if you
were tuned into the BBC. And if you missed even
three or four minutes of 'Blankety Blank', you
couldn't get it on 'catch-up' later.

Even if you were recording it on VHS, you had
to wait until 'Blankety Blank' was finished and
then 'wind' it back. Unless you'd noticed the time
into the video, it would be the moment you bought
your Vesta curry and Angel Delight back. That
meant you could spend ages rewinding the tape
back and forth until it jammed, as likely as not.

So, you would have to find something else to
watch on television, and TV in those days wasn't

all the Onedin Line. Oh no. Even if it was, (which it wasn't), you might be watching something with your girlfriend on the sofa, and if she said something to you, then you would have to take your mind off the Onedin Line and say something by way of reply. And if you didn't, you'd be in serious trouble.

Even if you were watching cricket, it wouldn't make any difference. I could go on about this sort of thing all night. And we didn't have remote controls either. So, if your vertical hold went and you got up to reach the knob at the back of the set and you forgot the tray in your lap, you'd have Vesta curry and Angel Delight all over the carpet.

Worst of all, if the girlfriend had moved to the armchair opposite the sofa because she couldn't stand the cricket, you'd have Vesta curry and Angel Delight all over her, and you'd certainly have to say something then or you'd be in even more serious trouble.

Finally, you'd hear that Boycott, during the melee, had just scored one more bringing him up to two. So, thanks to all that you'd have missed him getting off the mark.

Nowadays they don't know they're born!

THE END

The Humble Tale of Bernie Bear
Robert Blackthorne

"Hello? Is somebody there?" A strained voice drifted weakly through the gloom. The meagre shafts of light peeking through the solid wooden boards above scarcely managed to illuminate the area beneath.

The voice called out again.

"Hello? Can anyone hear me? I didn't mean to scare you. Please, it's been so long since I've had anyone to talk to."

From the depths of the dank surrounding space, behind the furthest sliver of light, a figure began to take shape. As the shadows faded from its edges, a roughly humanoid figure emerged. A pair of thick stumpy arms, a protruding rotund belly ending in a further duo of stumps, similar in proportion to the other limbs, all appeared splayed outward, without concern.

"Hello?" The voice called out once more.

"I could have sworn that someone was there?"

Eventually the darkness faded entirely from sight, and more of the speaker's features could be finally seen; they've yet to move, but the shape of their body and facial features are distinctly non-human, especially given the pair of rounded nubs which rest on the top of a strangely flattened head. Moreover, the outline seems oddly fuzzy ... sat as it is with its back up against the wall.

Is it covered in dust, or some kind of fur? Only further investigation will tell. With that thought, suddenly the surrounding space appeared to shift a little, pulling the observer forward to where the speaker is revealed. Funnily enough, as the dust re-settles, you notice that previous thoughts might well be proven true.

"Hello! So there you are. Nice to meet you ... I think?"

Sat on a small patch of stained wood with his back slumped against a dampened wall, was a dusty, furry, moth-eaten and mouldy-looking teddy bear.

"Oh, I'm sorry! I didn't mean that it *isn't* nice to meet you, it's just ... well, it's been so long since I've had a visitor of any kind, I'm not too sure what the difference is anymore ..."

The gleam in the stuffed bear's button eyes seemed to fade, but for only a moment, as it quickly began again.

"Oh goodness me, I forgot about my manners. They're quite important, you know. Well, since this is the first time we've met, I'd better tell you my name. It's Bernie. My name is Bernie Bear." The small stuffed creature proclaimed rather proudly.

"Well, I think it used to be 'Bernard', but nobody calls me that anymore. Nobody's called me much for a long time, come to think of it ..."

A brief pause and, after a small start of surprise, Bernie begins for a third time.

"Sorry, so sorry, I got lost in my thoughts for a moment there. Anyway, I might not have much to talk about right now. Besides, despite all the funny noises upstairs and my guesses as to what they might be, if you'd like, I can at least tell you the story of how I came to be here right now. That is of course should you wish to listen to it."

As Bernie finished speaking, the floor felt as if it were settling, almost as if a person may well be sinking into it. Then, despite the dimness of light and uncomfortably stuffy air, Bernie begins to recount his tale.

"Well, I guess the best thing to do would be to start with my earliest memory, okay?" he offered, hardly meaning what he said as a question.

"Well, there were a lot of confusing things at first, getting shoved this way and that. I remember some funny spinning things under me ... like rolling pins, as I and many others like me appeared to be riding them, one after the other in a long line.

Then, we were split up as we passed down a slope, until I got put in a little square box of some kind. It wasn't very big, but it had a nice clear opening to see out of; lots of things, all shapes and sizes passing by and far too much to take in at once.

However, I do remember seeing the silver and grey of the long whirring lines, and the blue of what I now know to have been gloved 'hands' fiddling with things around me as I travelled onward.

Anyway, by then I found myself stuffed into my box and placed in another, larger and stranger cage made out of the slightly thicker, brown stuff.

Sadly though, this cage blocked the view from my little window, and I could just barely hear the sounds of others like me close by. I tried talking to them, but maybe my hearing was too weak to make them out properly? At least I could feel them nearby. After a while, I heard a few voices discussing something about 'loading crates' before I rather unexpectedly felt myself rising into the air!

Next, after some bumps and a lot of loud noises, I found the cage we were all stuck in being ripped apart, and we were soon freed ... well, almost. One by one, I and the others were pulled out of this 'crate' and our boxes each placed on a nice, little platform.

This, I later learnt, was called a 'shelf'. Even though I knew the others were still all close by because nobody could move, all any of us could do was sit and watch. Watch and wait. Wait and see what the day might bring. Goodness, there was so much to learn just by watching people walk around. I mean, I could tell you it all, but that's not really the point of this story."

A moment of silence passed, interrupted briefly by the scuttling of a bug in the distance.

Bernie continued.

"Well, my part in things really comes to the fore when, on an otherwise normal day, I felt myself moving and quickly realised that something was shifting my little cage again. However, unlike the red-dotted face with gloved hands I saw before things went dark, there was a slim and softly rounded one looking down at me now.

Before I could think of much else, I was dropped, and with a small 'ksshh' hit the bottom of some even bigger, shinier cage. There were a lot of noises and movement after that, some things even dropped directly on me! Thankfully, before I knew it, I was shoved and pulled through some places which 'beeped' and 'dinged', and with so many new sounds and smells, I became quite dazed. The sudden thud beneath me quickly brought me back to my senses, which were alive in anticipation of what new event would be next. I heard much rumbling then until the feeling of movement came to an end.

Soon after that, I was hoisted upward, though I couldn't see very well through all the thin, white sheeting in front of me, I could still make out shadows, and new voices too. The first was sharp, happy and unfamiliar. This was a voice I would soon come to love, and the other I remembered as having a similar, gentle depth I had heard some hours before."

Suddenly, noises come from above. An amount of odd thudding here and there; the sounds of some murmuring, and shortly after, silence again. As quickly as he stopped, Bernie continued.

"Oh, sorry, that surprised me for a moment; you don't hear much around here anymore. Oh, right. Where was I? Yes, the moment I found 'home'. Ah ... not to get ahead of myself. You see, I still didn't know what was going on for a long while. I was taken by the thin-faced person and had my little cage wrapped in some kind of covering.

Then, for the remainder of that 'long while' I just mentioned, got to sit in some place quiet, and without much light. Just as I was getting bored, wondering if I wasn't better back where I'd come from, I felt things moving again. Within a few short moments I was placed in a much brighter and noisier place, despite my cage's covering, and could hear many voices, rather tunelessly, singing a simple song, which ended in a 'whooshing' noise, and a cheer.

Within a moment, there must have been much activity since I saw so many shadows pass by my small, shielded window out into the world."

The stuffed bear took another pause, somewhat more wistful this time. In fact, if a teddybear *could* smile, you'd almost swear that this one just did.

"Then, in the biggest shock of my life so far", Bernie continued. "I saw not just my covering, but the very cage holding me in place, hastily torn to shreds; a much smaller and rounder face than any I'd seen before now appeared, looking down at me. That was Little Sarah, and the first words I ever heard, before I even knew what words really were.

"Oh Mommy, he's so cute. I love him! He's such a nice little bear."

"I'm glad you like him sweetie", the thin faced person called 'Mommy' said, stepping towards the girl and then crouching over to embrace her whispering gently into her ear, before giving a little parting peck on the cheek

"Happy birthday Sarah."

"Sarah then began to squeeze me so hard between her arms and chest that I really thought I might burst, only for her to sit and cradle me gently as we looked quietly into one another's eyes. Then I realised that 'bursting' feeling never quite went away.

I felt it from inside for the rest of the night as she talked to me while we played together. Never before nor since the incident, have I felt quite so ... content."

A short pause followed, as if enjoying a sudden swathe of warm, familiar memories.

"We became fast friends, playing together many times after that. She had such a great imagination, did Sarah." the unmoving teddy bear now said, sounding much stronger than before. "We played all sorts of games where I was a hero saving a city from a terrible monster.

Though I knew the 'monster' fairly well, he was a monkey called Monty with mismatched buttons eyes, and he really wasn't so bad once you got to know him, despite his scary face. Since we sat next to each other on the dresser before bedtime ... Oh, I'm getting myself side-tracked again! Terribly sorry Monty, but I'll have to save your stories for later. Right now I need to finish the one about Sarah and how I ended up well... without her, I suppose ..."

Bernie trailed off, trying not to sound pained.

"Anyway, there was lots of fun and games, tea parties and such. I was usually asked to play 'Aunt Ethyl', always treated well and spoken for in a funny high-pitched voice, where Sarah always dragged out the 'o's in her words.

After meeting the big lady whose name I shared on that one cold holiday, I can see why. Oh, and the times we would play in the sandbox together, and dig for buried treasure or dinosaur bones, or even where I got to be king of whatever little sandcastle she made. Other times we were explorers, trying to find our way to lost cities, all in the jungle of our own backyard.

As I said, she had such an imagination ..."

Bernie's voice trailed off once more. A few more thumps and bumps interrupted the silence, followed by a loud metallic clang reverberated into nothing. After a long moment and waiting a further second, just to make sure he wouldn't be interrupted, Bernie continued, a new warmth settling into his voice.

"My days were spent from then on as little Sarah's closest companion and friend. We had no secrets and shared everything, even the blame for eating too many sweets before tea-time, because all of those wrappers couldn't *possibly* have been from her alone, you see.

That's how we spent our days; slaying dragons, saving people and their homes from monsters, discovering new things in the world around us, and practicing being 'grown-up' which everyone insisted little Sarah would soon become. How I wish I'd been there to see it, instead of ending up *here*..."

Berne took another thoughtful break from telling his story.

"Sadly, I think someone much cleverer than me once said 'all good things must come to an end'. The big man who Sarah called 'Daddy' mentioned it a lot. Well, especially after *the thing* happened, which really is what I need to get to!"

"I remember it being a cool day in spring, and everything was going on as normal until Sarah caught a bit of a cough. A few days later, as the weather got warmer, so did she, getting tired easily and coughing continuously. She ended up forced to stay in bed for a few days with something called a 'fever'. I stayed by her side the entire time of course," Bernie confirmed proudly.

"... or at least, as much of it as I could for sadly, during all her tossing and turning in bed, I got stuck down the side next to the wall.

'Nothing terrible,' I had thought at the time, but I was quite surprised by what happened next. See, little Sarah wanted to hold me again when she woke up, quite worried as to where I could be. I heard her daddy's voice offering to move the bed to find me, just like he'd done many times before.

The thing is, Sarah was simply too sick to get out of bed, so Daddy decided to move the bed with her still in it. That's where things went a little strange, as when I heard him heave and push the bed, some of the floor beneath me began to move too."

Bernie stopped for a moment.

"Even if I could have called out to them in that moment, it wouldn't have mattered. With the final, grunting push, the piece of floor I was on bent causing me to immediately fall backwards, away from the wall, and into this odd dark place.

I've not moved from this spot since and this is where you have come to meet me, whoever you are. May I say I'm glad of your company, even if you don't seem to be much of a talker yourself! Having someone to talk with makes a nice change from watching the bugs skitter by. I tried talking to them too, but they're not really very good listeners."

"Anyway," Bernie continued. "that's how I ended up down here, all by myself. The space isn't so bad, but it was all that came after my fall that worries me the most.

You see, even though I was fine, it's not like I could shout 'here I am', and since the floor had shifted itself back once the bed had been moved, Daddy had no way of finding me. He heaved and groaned for a while, before I heard his and Sarah's voices again.

Then there was more noise" he mumbled "but you tune it out after a while" a lot of grunting and scraping, and eventually the sound of Sarah crying. Her daddy offered some soothing reassurance:

'We'll find him, don't worry, just wait sweetheart.'

"Sadly though, they still haven't" Bernie finished reflectively. "It's been so long since I've seen her, or at least I think it has? I wasn't good at telling time to begin with, but there are no clocks down here. I wish I could find hope that they'll discover me soon, but honestly, I know the truth; they aren't even looking anymore."

The weight of his own words hit Bernie and his speech continued shakily.

"You see, after a long time of Sarah being upset, and her family trying to find me without much luck, they decided to make up a story. Since no-one knew what made me go missing." he muttered under his breath. "They decided to tell my little Sarah, that I had chosen to go away, to explore the world and learn new things, just like we did when we played together. They said that I even wrote and sent her a letter. And just when I thought they'd be caught out in a lie, I heard Sarah cry out again, though in joy this time, as she began to read aloud the letter I had apparently sent her.

At first, I was quite mad - really very angry that they had put these words in my mouth; I would never willingly leave my best friend, although I guess now it all was for the best. Little Sarah finally stopped crying herself to sleep, you see.

For a while at least, she would wonder aloud where I was now, and what I might be doing. Eventually, that too stopped, and the only thing to brighten up this lonely gloom was being able to hear her voice every now and then as she played or talked with friends who came to visit. Eventually I stopped being able to tell her voice from that of her Mommy. That was quite a while ago, and it's been quiet for some time since."

A crashing noise and two distinctly male voices then sounded from above, almost as if on cue.

"Well," Bernie followed on "It used to be ... "

"Unfortunately, my new little friend - if I may be so bold as to call you such - that is the end of my story. Or at least the one of how I ended up in this cramped and dusty space all by myself for goodness knows how long. Not much of an ending I'm afraid, but then, I never was much of a storyteller.

Still, I've grown used to this life now, even if it is a lonely one. Oh, to be able to see a face clearly and feel the warmth of their touch once more, that's all I really want. Sadly, short of a miracle, there's not much I can do about it. Sometimes you just get thrown into the unknown I guess, but there's probably a big difference between choosing to go away from everyone, wanting to live alone, and being forced to do so by chance. How strange though, to hear the people you love moving on around you, but never being able to see them again..." Bernie finished sadly, seeming to drift momentarily back into his own little world of isolation.

However, the stretching silence was suddenly cut short, as the banging above had not only restarted, but redoubled; the sounds of machines now blending into the irregular drumbeat of steps and male voices above. So many feet were now added to this chorus that dust had begun drifting down steadily all around, even covering poor Bernie in a fine layer.

"Ah, wonderful," he said "At least this should dry out the damp I've been sat in. I hope."

Then, as the machine noises drew ever closer, whirring, scraping, and grating their way around the room above, with a crash like a hammer blow, a piece of curved metal erupted through the low wooden plank ceiling.

With a heaving grunt and sharp crack, the beam a few feet away from Bernie's head was ripped asunder, light now pouring down in a shaft from above. Finally, the voices atop the light shaft could be heard clearly.

"Ok boss," a slight young man's voice announced. "Panel's up, but I think the wood rot goes further than we thought - all the way to that wall over there."

"What?" A much gruffer voice responded, "Oh for the love of Jim! Jim, get down and move your ladder, you'll have to paint later. Yes, *now* lad, before the floor gives way and you fall off of the damn thing." If Bernie had the ability, he would have held his breath at that point. Wood rot? What on earth was going on up there?

Before he could finish the thought, with another mighty slam the curved metal had once again reappeared, this time only inches from his teddy bear face. The wood above his head splintered and fell away above him, showering Bernie in debris, as the light shone down on him for the first time since his unfortunate fall from grace.

"Yeah boss, it's as bad as I thought. Throw me a bucket would you, and I'll ... huh?" The voice trailed off as the silhouette of a head appeared right above Bernie, whose button eyes were having difficulty adjusting to the newfound brightness of the room above. Suddenly, a hand descended into the muck and dust of the surrounding space, and gently pulled Bernie up ... up into brilliant light. Bernie had little idea what was happening at first, as the owner of both the hand and slight voice he'd heard already got the attention of those nearby, shouting:

"Hey guys, look what I found!" above the din.

The response was many wrinkled noses and some tutting in disgust. Bernie took a moment to take in the surrounding scene, wondering for the first time in a while where exactly he was since he didn't know any of these men, and little Sarah's belongings - her desk, her dresser, even her bed - were all somehow missing. The walls weren't even the same peachy colour they'd been before he had gotten lost. They were now a sort of light green.

Was this really still the same room he had once slept in? He barely had time to collect those thoughts before the gruff voice said to 'stop messing about and throw that thing out with the rest of the trash.' After which, Bernie felt himself inexplicably sailing through the air, and landing with a wet splat on top of a few stones and bits of wood at the bottom of what seemed to be a smooth, yellow-walled hole. 'Well,' Bernie thought, 'at least *this* is something different. I guess I got my wish. Ah well.'

Some additional broken bits of flooring were then dumped over poor old Bernie, and then some more, until the only thing sticking out of the rubble bucket was one his legs and an ear. Thankfully, things happened to not continue this way, as the drumbeats from a pair of light feet raced thunderously closer to all the others in the commotion.

"Wow!" a bright young voice chirped. "So this is going to be my room?" His query was followed almost immediately after by a woman's voice calling from a distance:

"Richard! You get back down here right now young man, there are men working up there!"
"Yeah, Moooom, I *know,* I just wanted to watch." The bright voice replied lightly.

"*Richard!*"

Then the gruff voice called out: "It's alright Ma'am, so long as he doesn't get in our way, he can stay by the door and watch. Any trouble and I'll send him straight down, alright?"

A moment's pause before the reply, "OK then,

But be *careful* up there, sweetie. We don't want anyone getting hurt!"

"I will, Mom!" ended the conversation ended, and, as the previous noise of construction workers resumed.

While careful not to disturb the men, Richard slowly walks around the room, studying their work, and inspecting the tools. When, to his great surprise, he sees something oddly familiar. It seems to be sticking out of a bucket of broken bits, but as he drew closer, there it was, sure as day, the leg of a teddy bear.

Bernie couldn't see anything at this point, stuck upside-down amongst a bunch of rotting wood chips and gravel, but he got quite the shock when he felt what he was *sure* was a small hand curl itself around his foot.

Gently it worked his leg back and forth, untill another hand joined him on his torso, and much like an uprooted carrot, he was hoisted back into the air.

"I knew it!" the young boy exclaimed, and the next thing Bernie heard was a wet squishing sound as Richard wrapped his arms around the bear's tiny sodden body in a tight embrace.

"Eh, what're you doing over there, son?" The gruff voice once again rang out. "What's that you've got?"

"I found this in the bin. Can I keep it please, Mister? Can I? Please?" a slight whine of uncertainty now creeping into the youth's voice.

"Oh, hey, Boss, isn't that the teddy I found?" the slight voice chimed in. "Well, we don't need it, so...." He let his voice trail off meaningfully.

"Really? You *want* that smelly old thing? Wouldn't you rather have a new one?" said the boss.

Bernie, now in the boy's arms, was able to see the large, bearded man raising his eyebrows from over the shoulder he was being pressed against.

"Yeah!" shouted Richard, turning enthusiastically. "He just needs a good wash, I think. Anyway, what about finders keepers? He's still good, even if he is a little wet and smelly."

At this point, a woman's figure rounded the door, arms folded but with just the slightest of smirks on her face. Then, while pretending to sound angry, she exclaimed "Richard, didn't I *just* tell you not to bother these nice men? What's all this fuss over anyway?" a false air of ignorance in her tone.

"Mom, Mom! Look what I found," he said, presenting Bernie proudly up towards her chest. "That means I get to keep him, right? I mean ... if that's ok with everyone else," he said shyly, turning to address the room.

"No problem," "no skin off our noses" and "surething kiddo" was the general chorus of reply.

"Oh, fine then," said Richard's mother, tapping one finger across folded arms, her smirk still as strong as the mock anger in her tone. "So long as it gets you out from under the workmen's feet while they fix up your new room, OK son?"

"Yeah!" he exclaimed excitedly, rushing forward and hugging her legs, "Thanks, Mom, I love you!" He disappeared behind her and out of the door just as quickly as he came, a soggy Bernie now flopping in tow.

That's where Bernie found himself, after surviving the horrors of what he later found was called 'the washing machine', before being strung out to dry, and then sat on a warm radiator for a bit, he really just felt quite stunned.

It wasn't until a few days later, once the workmen had gone and he was finally reunited with little Richard that everything started to make sense. As they lay there, snuggled in his bed in the same room Bernie had always lived in (well *under*), things finally felt right again.

"Goodnight, Mom" Richard mumbled as she kissed his forehead, and thanks again for letting me keep him," he finished sleepily, cuddling his new best stuffed friend with a sigh. Quietly and softly came her reply, looking back as her hand rested on the door frame.

"Of course, sweetie, He's such a nice little bear."

THE END

Fruit, Bacteria at a pinch, but no Bears
Chris Robinson

No, it's what I do all the time. If you're established as a regular, then it's regular work. There are about seven or eight of us regulars. The others always see it as infra dig; on their way to better things. I don't see them as better things, if indeed they do get them, which of course they don't. The way I see it, Hamlet is a liquorice all-sort without words.

As for mammals, I'm all right with mammals. Except that I draw the line at bears. I'll come to that later. What about fruit? Well, fruit is variable. I'm <u>the</u> blackcurrant you know, the big one who can just manage to squash himself down the neck of the bottle. Well, it's just padding of course, though one has to push a bit then plop into the swimming pool. They do it all with computers now, though it was lashings of purple dye when I started. I'm surprised it's still running.

Bananas depend on what they want you to do. If you've got to run, you need to have the inside of the curve at the front; the other way round is not on. Once this clever-sticks director insisted on the inside curve at the back. I don't know the reason why, but the outside of the curve forwards it was. He said it wouldn't work otherwise.

It was me that wouldn't work. For one thing, you can't see where you're going. I ran into a raspberry first. Then I knocked two greengages over. In the end they had to clear the set, and have me run backwards but my shoes were pointing the wrong way, weren't they? I mean, what does it matter? Why can't a banana run backwards like anyone else? Anyway, there was a scene, I mean social rather than dramatic, and I don't know what happened after that you don't ask, do you?

However, the next one you may remember, starting with me leaning over a balcony watching the tangerine dancing to the Habanera from Carmen. Just finished the latest one; it isn't out yet. I'm stuck in a ticket barrier at a station, trying to catch the Fruit Salad Express. Because I'm recessed in the middle, the electric eye thinks I'm already through when I'm not, and it's snapped shut pinching me in the midriff. No harm done; padding like the blackcurrant. The other fruit are trying to get me out. A pineapple is pulling at my legs and an apricot is trying to push my chest back while a strawberry's run off for help.

Confectionery is all right. I spent five years as a liquorice twist in you-know-what, but I recently got promoted to the lead; you know, the orange, black and white square one. There's not so much acting in confectionery; more acrobatics really, or just juggling. Falling out of a packet is a bit scary at first, but you soon get used to it.

I'm up for anything. In fact, you have to be. Anything ... animal, vegetable, mineral ... except, in my case, bacteria. OK, its extra pay, but it's just not me. Health and safety have had their eye on bacteria for quite a while. That's how I got the lead liquorice allsort. My mate Fred accepted a bacterium but not without misgivings I heard, as he is somewhat accident-prone. You'll have seen it, it's still on. Germs having a cocktail party in the lime-scale; girl in tight jeans bends over and squirts them with Lavvo. Then she pulls the chain, so to speak. That's the bit. They'd never seen anything like it. I'm not surprised they've finally banned flushing. I mean we can all die a death twitching, if that's what they want. They don't need Laurence Olivier as Richard III, do they? Though that's what they generally get. All you require is the squirt. You don't need a tidal wave as well.

He's out of hospital now, anyway. I visited him last Tuesday. I planned to bring him a bunch of grapes but then I remembered his nasty accident when he was the first sultana in the cake mix dancing on ice. I couldn't take him chocolates because he was once fully wrapped in silver paper when the fire alarm went off.

It was only a practice, as it happened. Still, two hours encased in tinfoil is a long time. I couldn't even get out of his matching depression in the plastic tray. Good job they'd cut him a slit for breathing. So, I took him a bunch of flowers instead.

That was where Fred and I met; at the Daffodil Dairy Spread. We were the two flowers looking over the girl's shoulder when she was eating the sandwich at the picnic. The first one was a pair of daffodils, but there were complaints that the spread didn't contain daffodils.

It seemed daft to me: I mean you can look at something without it being made of you. Anyway, they did it again with Fred and I as sunflowers.

Sunflower oil, get it? We had to stand up straighter; it wouldn't have been a problem, except that it took all day to shoot. The girl was great but the lad beside her kept picking his nose. On about take thirty-three, Fred picked his nose for a laugh if you ever feel a bit down, imagine a sunflower picking its nose but it turned out the boy had got it right for the first time. The director went off his head, but computer you-know-what had just come in, and they put an earlier Fred in place of the last one.

I was talking about mammals, wasn't I? Why do I draw the line with bears? Winnie the Pooh is fine, you might think, since that is obviously what I'm doing now. I hope you realise that. I'm not just any bear, I'm Winnie the Pooh. There's not much point if you didn't. But there's more to this bear than meets the eye.

There are depths, and it's not just Pooh Bear. Oh no. I can tell you that I've also done Rupert. Yes, Rupert. It was a long time ago, I have to admit.

It was the same routine, same film or musical or other; same idea using public transport, platform-pavement stuff, that sort of thing. I stood by one of the entrances to Piccadilly Circus tube station. One arm elevated almost vertically, in a stiff sort of wave as I shuffled around on my feet, looking like I'm on a turntable. I looked a bit like Ted Heath outside Downing Street when he won that election some years ago.

They had already bought a ticket for me from the machine. My trousers didn't have any pockets you see, which I suppose Rupert's did, or rather do, since I don't know where he keeps his money otherwise. He might have a sporran in his underpants.

What made me think of that was one of my mates doing Braveheart Porridge Oats when they put his costume on back to front. Anyway, now I'm going down the escalator, no wave of course, just looking straight ahead; everything perfectly normal for me. Trouble was, especially as it was rush hour, everything was perfectly normal for everyone else. When I was about half way down, I heard one kid's voice below: "Look, mummy, there's Rupert." Then something like "Shush, dear, don't point. It's rude to stare."

That was that. I've never felt so isolated in my life. Worse was to come. Standing on the platform, someone brushed past me. "Sorry!" he said, just as if I were anyone else. Then into the train somebody said "after you" as we got in together. I went to one of the seats where you sit with your back to the window facing each other, or rather, facing a row of newspapers apart from one of them, directly opposite me, who was reading a book.

She looked at me for all of half a second, smiled thinly as if she'd remembered a joke somebody had told her twenty years ago, and went back to reading something that was obviously not a Rupert book.

For the first time in my life, I knew what it was like to be completely alone. Station after station passed. Just after the doors had closed for the fourth (or was it fifth time?), the chap next to me shuffled a little, and I heard him whisper into my ear aperture, "Just passing through, are you?" He couldn't see me smile, of course. All I could do was nod twice, I hoped thoughtfully. I flatter myself that it was a thoughtful nod. I remembered that when I was doing the rhubarb stalk and being advised by Sammy the Slug in the Horticultural and General Insurance series, the director singled out my thoughtful nod for praise.

He got out at the next stop. "Best of luck," he whispered as he passed. All I could manage was a brisk, eager nod. Then I was all by myself again, the overpowering feeling of just passing through defining what we're experiencing, I suppose, though I've never felt so alone in the process of actually doing it. I made a mental note for future reference: 'no more bears' ... or words to that effect.

So why am I doing Pooh? Well, perhaps my Rupert was appreciated, and perhaps that was why they asked me. Being in a niche business, if I might call it that, it doesn't do to risk disappointing someone who appreciates your talent, does it? I have to add that an extremely large gas bill had arrived through my letterbox on the same day, but I have to assure you it's mainly the creative challenge that drives me on.

There's something intensely lonely about being a bear. Why do I feel more part of the human race as a custard cream, or a blackcurrant? Perhaps it's because you don't ask a custard cream or a blackcurrant if they're just passing through.

They're calling me. I'll have to go now. It's been really nice meeting you. May I shake your paw? Oh, it's the other way round, isn't it? Hope you think of me when you see the orange and black square one. Remember, just as there's something of everyone in Hamlet, we're all this-and-that square ones in our own way. Funny old world, isn't it? As they say, it takes all sorts...

And don't forget the sunflower picking its nose!

THE END

Involuntary Isolation
Irene Styles

Gravel crunched under my feet as the path curved around the bushes to a white painted window. Stopping and peering in, I could see the room was empty. I leant against the frame. The glass was smooth and cold on my forehead. The earlier rain had stopped and, looking up, I could see patches of blue pushing through the grey clouds.

I knew this view of the room so well. It was the only view I had been able to see for weeks; a single bed, a wardrobe, a small table and two armchairs. It would be comfy enough, but not home, not her home.

Oh yes, I had tried to soften it with her favourite photos, pretty throws and her precious nick-knacks, all displayed neatly around the room, but it was still not home.

At first, she had cried and begged me to take her back home, but for her own safety, I knew that was the one thing I could not do. Over the months, the crying had lessened. She accepted, because she had forgotten.

I turned to face the garden. The gentle breeze stirred the leaves of the blue rhododendron bushes and on the lawn, out of the shade, the odd dandelion stood, defiant in its right to grow there.

A soft tapping from inside the window made me spin around and a blue, uniformed lady spoke loudly through the glass and her face mask, making sure I could hear her.

"Here's your mother, Mrs. Roberts. She's well and so pleased to see you."

I knew that was a kind, white lie. How can a person with a rotting brain disease be well, or pleased to see you? She wouldn't even have remembered you were visiting. But I knew what she meant, and I appreciated the pretence.

I nodded and smiled at her as she positioned the wheelchair in front of the window and left the room.

"Hello, mum." I gushed. My voice, sounding light and happy, hid the heaviness of my heart.

There was no response. The slight, grey haired lady remained silent and motionless in her chair. She looked frail and so alone, I wanted so much to wrap her in my arms and tell her everything was ok and that I loved her, that her family loved her.

Damn this evil virus. She had been served a double whammy. Deterioration of her mental health took her away from us and everything she knew and remembered. And now the isolation imposed upon her and our family for weeks had caused the dementia to accelerate, her mind becoming more of an empty room with fewer and fewer memories.

Before the pandemic, some days had been good and for a while her eyes would come alive and she remembered who I was, other days her eyes were dull, her face blank and I was a stranger to her. Back then at least I could shower her with love, hug her and make sure she was comfortable, but Covid had taken that from us.

Yes, rules are rules, and they were put into place for everyone's safety, especially the old and vulnerable, but it was a bitter blow. I knew that several of the elderly residents here had passed away alone. Relatives had been forbidden to see their loved ones as they took their last breath. No goodbyes and no decent send-offs to bring closure. How sad and lonely for all concerned.

Now I can only talk to her, regardless that my whispers through the windowpane fall on unhearing ears. There is no remembering. She lives alone, within herself. There is no comfort-bringing release from her isolation.

I chatter incessantly filling the emptiness and sometimes, something I say resonates with her and I can see it has sparked some memory within her empty world.

Occasionally I would bring along old photographs of her and dad, me as a child, pictures of our old dogs, of Gran and Grandad. Black and white photos from long ago, and sometimes when she saw them, her eyes would flash with recognition and she would smile but the talking, the conversations, had long stopped.

I imagine her world as a big empty house, with a single chair, on which she sits alone and each door leading to the rooms of this house, full of her memories, her personality, is locked and she cannot reach out to turn the key and enter those rooms. She can only sit in isolation and emptiness.

My time is up. I press my lips to the window, leaving a red outlined imprint. I mouth, "I love you".

As I walk away, I turn and wave. Her face still

staring through the pane, sometimes, I think, she has finally seen me, and she smiles. Or is that just wishful thinking on my part?

Over the coming weeks I saw my mother slowly deteriorating. Then one night the phone rang. The call I had dreaded for so long.

"Mrs. Roberts, I'm so sorry to have to tell you, your mum passed away this evening. It was very peaceful."

I put down the phone, knowing there would be no more sleep for me that night. My husband Jim, sat up in bed and realised at once when he saw my face. I went to the kitchen and brewed a pot of tea. Jim joined me but I told him to go back to bed, I needed to think about what had just happened and what had to be done next.

Sadly, not much. No service, no flowers, just my mum in a box, stored in a freezer until there was room for a cremation. This thought set my tears flowing, my chest heaved as I gasped for breath.

"Oh mum, this is not what I wanted for you." I sobbed.

Now it was my turn to be alone, alone in my grief.

THE END

Last Words
John Blackbird

Date: April 15th 1917.
Location: Somewhere in the North Sea.
Time: Between One to Two AM.

I never thought I'd die like this, curled up like a baby in a rocking cradle. Only, I'm not a baby. I'm an able seaman; a man of twenty-four, wrapped up in sheets of torn linen, in a lifeboat of which I am the sole occupant.

I'll try to keep the details of my situation short, because I only have a few dry scraps of sketch paper and a single lead pencil. I will have to ration my limited resources, as I have tried to do with depleting physical and mental energy for most of the night so far.

Unfortunately, as time slips by, my personal chances of survival have significantly decreased, with the weather becoming more and more hostile to human life as I witness examples of nature's cruelty, which I'll try to explain later. That particular part of this story is too raw right now.

It's still unclear to me what exactly happened, but I'll endeavor to recount as best I can limited by the light of the moon and the decreasing dexterity of my frost-bitten hands. These may be the last words I ever speak or write in this life.

A few days ago, (April 10th to be precise.) we set out as part of a small flotilla of British minesweeping vessels, patrolling the Dogger Bank on the North Sea. Our ship, HMS Lir, was a fishing trawler converted for war service. She was a good-sized vessel, manned by a crew of ten.

This expedition was part of a response to reports of increased German naval activity within the area. I guess since the announcement of the Americans joining the war the previous week, the Kaiser must have ordered the unrestricted resumption of their U-boat attacks.

Throughout this war, nothing scared me more than stories of the U-boats. Like ghosts they strike without you ever seeing them, eventually surfacing to obliterate anything and everything they decide to send to the bottom of the sea. Then they slip quietly away under the waves, like merciless mechanical sea serpents.

I believe that tonight, I and my fellow crewmates ran afoul of the damn things! I can't be certain, but I'm convinced enough those sly bastards got us!

It was around twenty-three hundred and thirty hours (23:30pm), on the 14th of April when it happened. Our ship, HMS Lir, was trailing behind the rest of the flotilla. This was because we were having engine problems and, as a result, we slowed down to position ourselves at the back of the patrol.

I was checking the condition of the sweeper wires, near the stern at the time. I don't remember much of the attack; just the initial impact and then the fire and smoke as the first torpedo struck our starboard side.

The sudden ear-bursting explosion made the whole ship tremble. A flash of burning red and yellow blinded me, blurring my vision. I think I collapsed on the deck at that point … hitting my head.

Everything turned into an unclear silhouette of black and grey, with the odd flash of reddish yellow. A sharp throbbing pain radiated around my head as well as the unbearable tinnitus ring echoing in my ears. I crawled out on the cold, hard, deck; calling out for help, but no one came. Very quickly I found myself unable to breathe effectively as the melting metal and toxic clouds of burning fuel suffocated my lungs.

Everything happened so fast, and I don't believe our Commander, or any other members of the crew, had a chance to announce, *"Abandon ship!"*

I think I must have managed to get to my feet, feeling around and eventually finding the deck rail. Then … the second torpedo struck! The ship rattled violently again, knocking me over the side and into silence and complete darkness.

Sometime later I woke up to the sensation of being thrashed violently from side-to-side on a hard wooden surface; a whooshing and swirling of water and beating wind over the sound of creaking wood. My eyes stung, adjusting gradually to what little light there was. Black smoke clouds overhead had blocked out the moonlight. I looked out to survey my surroundings; I was met with nothing, just an endless nothing atop jet-black water. There was no sign of the ship, no sign of the others and no sign of the enemy. I was completely alone!

Suddenly, to my complete surprise I heard the sound of a voice being carried on the air; the cry sounding more like the moans and groans of an animal in pain, but, this sound was no animal; there was definitely a man out there … somewhere!

The relief in my heart was great, knowing then that I was not alone. But then my mind began to conjure up concerns. My short-lived relief gave way to dread. Questions came up in my mind. Who was out there? Why were they out there? Were they hurt and in need of help? The more important question to me though ...were they friend or foe?

Taking a chance, I reluctantly called out. The response was faint, an unintelligible echo. Calling out again, the response was delayed and the caller evidently sounding in a degree of pain.

"Help...he'...help!" The voice grew fainter with each reply to my desperate shouts.

"Thank God!" I thought. The response was in English. This was likely one of the 'Lir's' crew. With little time, and energy to waste, I plunged my hands into the sharp icy water, paddling in the direction of the voice, calling out to him, to help guide me to his location. The moon still hid behind a thick black curtain of cloud. I was still effectively navigating blind.

"Hey! Hey out there! Keep talking. Say something. I'll find you! Just keep making noise! Slap your

hands or legs in the water if you have to!"

I shouted, pleaded, repeated over and over again but with little result!

Minutes felt like hours. For about ten minutes, the longest ten minutes of my damn life, I paddled; hands painfully red-raw with the attacking sensation of the water, like small cuts to the bone without breaking the skin.

The mystery survivor's voice slowly fell silent; possibly drowned I thought, another sad victim of this bloody chess game called war.

I stopped searching, my heart and spirit completely depressed, my mind now numb.

I curled up in a ball on the lifeboat floor, clutching at torn rags of grey linen for what little warmth I could salvage.

Time passed, I don't know how much. I was now completely exhausted and trying desperately to stay awake, even slapping myself in the face hoping the infliction would be enough to stop me from drifting off. As much as my mind and body cried out for the blessed relief of sleep, I knew if I gave in … I'd never wake up again.

But then, in a turn of amazing luck, the moon finally unveiled itself, its pale face began to break through the veil of clouds, lighting up the area enough for me to see a loose collection of floating wreckage, about forty meters north of me. I plunged my hands into the icy sea once more and paddled and paddled for dear life itself.

Once I got close enough to the wreckage, it became quite clear what it was. My eyes confirmed what my ears and my heart suspected: a cluster of bodies, five to be exact, gathered around the timber scraps of a lifeboat. One body aboard showed as mortally wounded. As for the rest ... they were gathered around, held close together and shoulder deep in the sea, floating on the surface like sea buoys. No one appeared to be moving, with not the faintest fog of breath in the cold air escaping from any single of them.

My burning red and blistered hands were painful; but, not as painful as the numbness that overtakes you when you've failed to save your fallen and injured pals. I knew them. Good lads to a man. They were the Lir's crew, or what was left of it. As for the other four, I'm afraid I never came across them. If they are out there, I hope to see them again and that they are faring better than me.

The one that stuck out to me the most was the young lad on the wreck, mostly because he was new to our crew. I don't remember much of his personal story beyond that he was a fresh-faced Scot, eighteen years old, newly married with a family somewhere in Scotland.

He must have received a beating in the attack from those torpedoes, as he was evidently worse off than the others. His left arm and leg were missing, blood spilling into the water, diluting the blackness as the dark red reflected off the moonlight. His once warm and youthful cheeky face now remained frozen, still and somber. He was clutching something to his breast tightly with his remaining right arm.

I regret to confess this part.

Once I realized that they had all perished, I decided to loot the bodies for anything useful that could sustain my own survival. The task was daunting beyond words; patting down the stiff and frigid remains of my pals for anything from food to lighters. Even with any personal items to keep safe to take home to their families, they would stand a better chance to keep preserved on this boat than in the water ... or that at least was my reasoning.

The young Scot had a sketchbook on him with a pencil. In fact, that's what I'm writing this tale of sorrow on; with the dry pages he had on his person. With that done, I simply drifted away and left, deciding to write this whole event down or at least my account of this night.

I waited and drifted, trying desperately to keep my mind off the wild northern winds; hoping beyond hope that the sun would come up soon. At the moment all I have is the moonlight for company, and she is a quite cold companion.

That's as much of tonight as I can account for up to this point. All I can do now, I guess, is pray it doesn't rain, hold on and survive until dawn.

I don't know what use or purpose this record may serve. If it survives me, I hope whoever finds these pages will have a better understanding of what happened out here tonight.

The rain persists; soaked to the bones. Can't keep warm; can't stop the shivers.

Hands and feet are now chalk-white and turning coal-black. No feeling left; at least the pain is gone. Darkness slowly turning grey. Exhausted!

Want to shut my eyes. Painful not to; desperate not to; I don't know if it's a real or a sea-born mirage as my vision is fading again. There are voices on the air again; not the pleadings or the reassurances of strangers trying to salvage what's left of me. Familiar whispers. Comforting; loving voices of familiarity. Mother! Father! Are you out here too?

There came a light, bright as shining sunflowers, almost angelic as a summer morning sunrise.

Is this what heaven looks like?

I'm in God's hands now.

THE END

Red Card
Colin Dunn

I sit here in the isolation of the changing room reflecting on the choices I made over the season, my team mates long gone but even they don't know the full story of what I have done, or the reasons behind it, but don't be too quick to judge.

This is a story of greed, betrayal and of highs and lows. Am I sorry for what I have done? Possibly! Would I do it again? Maybe! But there are good reasons for it, which is more than a simple goalkeeping mistake which got me sent off today.

I need to start from the beginning, though for you to understand, this story both begins and ends with the Derby, with City.

It all started in August when I was given the Number 25 shirt and my first full season as a professional. I had broken into the first team towards the end of the previous season and was a sub a few times where I was given number 30 in the squad. Seeing Jackson 25 made me happy at the time.

I knew it would be difficult to get playing time but once I had played a few times something snapped in my brain. Even better, I felt like a celebrity: an interview with the local media, I got featured on Football Focus and was even included in the FIFA video games. Life definitely felt good.

It was mid August when I was asked to play due to Robert Jones getting injured while playing for Wales, and David Saxon not at full health. I remember that day well as Karl Parker, the manager, called me into the office and asked if I was ready to play the following night in a game broadcast live on Sky Sports. "Hell, Yes!" I said jumping for joy.

It was a tough game, and I made some great saves including saving a penalty but City beat us 3-2. I made several more appearances but as soon as David and Robert were fit again I lost my place. Karl explained with David retiring at the end of the season, I would be given a new contract and be sent on loan once the transfer window opened in January. I didn't know then what was about to happen though.

There had always been tension between Karl and the owners, but it reached boiling point in November. There were rumours Karl had gone to the board of directors to ask for a bigger transfer budget and there were arguments. He somehow managed to keep his job, but they were looking for any excuse to get rid though.

A few days later that excuse came as we narrowly got beat 1-0 in the FA cup. This despite them scoring a freak goal in the last minute of the match, but Karl was sacked that night. I remember that weekend well I was happy being on the bench; it was also the weekend my life started to fall apart.

No one knew I had a gambling problem. I was

in small debt but managing with the wage and meagre savings I had, plus I was on a winning streak, winning over 50 grand in the last few months.

I wouldn't say I had a serious problem, as I stuck to what I would call minor gambling like small bets, the lottery and scratch cards, however I was starting to build up a debt.

I knew I could handle that; the gambling, what was happening at the club and a divorce after only a year that would cause any 19-year-old to go crazy, but worse was yet to come.

It was always a mistake to get married when I did. I had only known Lia for around six months at that time but thought she was the one. However it was a disaster from the start. Princess Lia, I used to call her, after the Star Wars character, which she hated as she knew felt Princess Lia was spoilt.

It was a year of mostly arguing, but once I had got the professional contract things had calmed down or so it seemed. She admitted cheating on me with a team mate. She told me that very weekend Karl was sacked, and she left the house to stay with family.

Within a week, Donald Franks was announced as manager and things got a lot worse. During his playing career Don was known as a hard man who would often be sent off: he was also known as a bully getting sacked just months before as a coach at Sunderland.

I had a terrible feeling about him, and on his second day there he called me into the office and told me I had no future at the club and he would finish me. I took no notice but did start drinking a lot more. Then December came and things became even worse.

It was the week before Christmas and Don had invited Castro a Brazilian defender who had been suspended for the past six months for violent conduct, to train with a view to signing him. It was that first training session with him that it happened. Don decided to do a training match First team versus reserves with Castro playing a defensive midfielder role for the first team.

It was during a corner that he went feet first on me. I still can't remember what happened, but I was on the ground with a broken arm and a possible fractured leg. It was merry fucking Christmas indeed as I would be out for more or less the rest of the season and my career possibly over.

I can't prove anything, but I know Don and Castro had a conversation before that training match, and I know they glanced in my direction.

I spent several months out doing what I could to get back to full fitness helped by one of the few friends I had left. It was a tough six months but I worked hard on my fitness and by mid April I had played a few matches for the reserves again.

I knew Don had tried to end my contract, but the club didn't want to spend thousands on a pay out for me and preferred to just let my contract run out, which worked perfectly in my favour.

So, we came to May and the final match of the season. Since Don had been manager, the club had slip down the table needing a win by three goals to avoid relegation. I knew the fans wanted the owners gone and I felt relegation would spell the end of Don's career.

I broke every rule in the book by betting on the club losing by using my friend's account. They even helped me to set up a plan.

If the club lost, I would win £250, 000 - enough to pay off the divorce settlement agreed with Lia and to live comfortably while looking for a new club. Yes, you might think it's greedy, but I think it more than justified.

So, the plan was simple I needed to play this final match. One obstacle was out of the way as Saxon was now officially retired after getting a hamstring injury during the previous match. I just needed to find a way to get John out of the way, something I still feel guilty about as he was one of the few first-time players to look out for me. The plan worked perfectly though.

All players at the club had a pre-match meal the night before so sitting next to him I managed to slip a laxative into his meal.

John would have an uncomfortable night and as I had assumed, I was reluctantly named in the starting lineup. So far so good. One thing I had not counted on though was us making a good start.

I had always intended to play the full ninety minutes but for the first time in months the team played as though their lives depended on it. Within five minutes we had scored, within ten we were 2-0 up. This was certainly not going to plan, but finally City had a chance, and my limited acting skills were brought into action as I pretended to dive for the ball and let it past my fingertips into the goal.

To anyone watching I hoped it looked as if I was just unfortunate. Things started to turn as tempers began to flare up and a few disagreements between players happened.

One of these was to be with Castro who made a clumsy challenge conceding a penalty. Arguments erupted and he headbutted the player with the ref sending him straight off.

Obviously I pretended to save by deliberately diving the wrong way, but at half time the score was 2-2 and I was confident my plan would still work.

So on to the second half, and once again I started to get nervous as we had chance after chance, City then had a player sent off, which equalled things up. I had to do something, so I did.

It was now seventy five minutes of the match played and only fifteen remaining so when I seen City number nine heading towards me, I rushed towards him and did a deliberate two-footed tackle.

Don had used all substitutions by this point so one of my teammates already on the pitch would have to replace me. I would have completely weakened the side.

Sure enough, the referee came over and gave me an instant red card. I looked over and their number nine, despite seconds earlier rolling about as though he had been shot, was already back up on his feet.

I didn't see which of my team mates replaced me in goal. As far as I was concerned they could all go to hell, not one of them supported me or asked how I was over the last six months.

They were too busy being selfish and I could never forgive them anyway especially since one of them was now dating Lia.

I went back into the changing room and showered. I should have felt guilt or something, but I could feel nothing but relief that this was all over. I got dressed as I heard the away fans cheering not once but four times. City had won 7-3.

I had done it; my revenge on the club, on my team mates and on Don was complete. United are relegated and I couldn't care less. Don told me he would finish me, but it feels great to know I am the one who has finished him.

All the team are long gone now, and so am I as this story should be getting burnt into the night sky on a lantern.

This was my story though of why, over twelve months I went from the highs to the very lows. I don't know what my future holds but I do know after today while it might not be in football, but one thing is for certain ... the name Ben Jackson will never be forgotten at United!

THE END

Right Up Scrooge's Street
Chris Robinson

The tale of how Scrooge finally realised he really had reformed.

Of the lost - which is to say abandoned - stations on the London underground, it is Scrooge Street which is perhaps the most likely to be haunted, if you believe in these things. It lies on a disused offshoot of the City branch of the Northern Line, and was built to serve the vast numbers of workers at the house of Scrooge and Marley, which prospered far more after Scrooge's repentance of his miserly ways than it ever did before it. Dickens would have naturally missed this part of the story out, Christmas being no time for emphasising the materially enriching possibilities of goodness.

Eventually the firm was obliged to build new offices elsewhere, and the old premises were knocked down. In their place, Scrooge built a row of neat and comfortable houses; one for himself, another for his clerk Bob Cratchit, and the rest given to long-standing employees who had served the firm in the early years of its great expansion.

In more recent times, the land on which the street stands has been much coveted by property developers, who have been prepared to offer vast sums of money for the plot, but those who live there now are protected by the provision in

Scrooge's will, that the road through it must be named after him in perpetuity; and the authorities in the City, mindful also of the tourist trade, have refused to consider any challenge to this. Since no bank or other financial institution would be seen dead with a head office in Scrooge Street, the immunity from upheaval the inhabitants enjoy is complete.

Immediately next to the covered-up top of the lift shaft at the station was a small patch of land that had for many years, been Scrooge's garden. In his miserly days he had sown it with oats for his porridge, and paid his clerk Bob to reap the grain with a pair of office scissors; these were then crushed in small batches in the office's copying press, and after several days' gruelling labour, enough porridge oats resulted to provide Scrooge with about a week's worth of breakfasts (hot) and suppers (cold).

It was the reformed Scrooge's decision to cultivate something else, such as sunflowers and pansies and wallflowers and grass for the children, in his newly acquired, or rather newly recognised, extended family to enjoy and play in.

It was indeed in the release of Bob Cratchit to more conventional clerical activities that Bob's business genius first found its way into practice; the rapid growth of Scrooge and Marley thereafter owing a great deal to this.

One winter's day Scrooge's nephew's oldest boy, aged ten or eleven, an active, practical lad named Tom, deciding to plant a sunflower seed the following spring, and dibbing a small hole on an exploratory basis, found an unexpected resistance in the earth, and, enlarging the hole, discovered a coin. He showed this to Scrooge, who saw at once it was not a British coin, something with which he was familiar. Scrooge therefore took the boy with him to the newly established British Museum and the coin was identified as Roman.

"If we dig a hole," Tom said excitedly, "... we might find some more coins."

"I'm not so sure about that," Scrooge replied, not wanting to have anything to do with digging for treasure, since the activity of grubbing for money, in the literal sense, was not a thing he wanted to encourage in the boy. He was also disinclined to try himself as the activity reminded him of his shameful past.

There is nothing like the scepticism of an adult to encourage activity in a child, and it was, therefor, hardly surprising that about a week later, when Tom visited his father's uncle again, and while Scrooge was busy baking a chocolate cake for their tea, the lad abstracted a spade from the garden shed and set to work.

Nature in the form or wind, rain, earthworms and birds had already eroded the hole made by the dibber so much that only a small depression marked the place where the coin had lain buried. It was, however, just recognisable, and no sooner had the spade cut into the soil beside it, further resistance prevented it digging any deeper.

A few seconds later a veritable hoard of coins began to appear. Tom ran to Scrooge, who was just removing the cake from its tin.

The reformed Scrooge was far too amiable to

be angry when the boy told him the news of his discovery, and undertook to examine the new 'find' as soon as he had tested the cake with a knife. When the cake proved to be as easy to slice into as the earth in the garden had not been, he followed the boy as he eagerly scampered ahead.

The coins at the edge of the pile were somewhat scattered, and it took them some time, taking turns with the spade, to extract what seemed to be the last one. Dark had indeed begun to fall when it was placed in the wheelbarrow along with the rest.

"I'll have to go now, uncle," said Tom.

He called Scrooge uncle, since 'great-uncle' was too much of a mouthful, especially when the mouth in question was usually full of things like chocolate cake in Scrooge's presence.

Tom took another slice of cake and left.

Scrooge remembered that they had not put the spade away, and carefully made his way through the dark to where they had left it, just beside the hole.

As he carried the spade, still caked with earth, to the shed, it happened to pass through a shaft of light thrown by the kitchen window. It goes without saying that the lights in Scrooge's house were particularly bright nowadays and in that light, Scrooge saw a round shape protruding from the earth still attached to the spade. It was another coin.

As soon as Scrooge had abstracted it, he heard a loud moan, and, to his horror, the first horror he had felt since his reformation, he saw a bright but somewhat sickly light emanating from the hole where the coins had been.

He had seen that light before; it was the ghastly light of the underworld, the light which had surrounded the first ghost he had seen on that unforgettable night, only a few years ago in fact, but which now seemed to him to be a lifetime away.

He was, therefore, not surprised when another, even louder, moan came from below. He was, however, deeply shocked and indeed horrified.

The same emotions he felt, only even more strongly, when a ghostly figure appeared from the hole, rising but with no apparent sense of liberation. Indeed, the figure seemed positively unwilling to elevate itself.

Although it had passed through a hole in the ground, Scrooge was not surprised to observe that its clothing was clean. He should not perhaps have been surprised that the clothing in this case was a toga, but he was nevertheless.

Scrooge's previous experience of ghosts had been associated with a sense of guilt, but he felt no such pangs on this occasion, since the discovery of the coins had been by chance, and in the course of making his garden available to his great-nephew. In these circumstances, he thought himself justified in not making any enquiries of the ghost to begin with, and to wait for the man in the sickly, greenish, luminous toga to state whatever his business was first.

The silence lasted longer than Scrooge was comfortable with, but the spirit finally spoke.

"I am the ghost of Iacobus Marlius," the spectre announced.

"Excuse me," Scrooge began, "but you don't much look like the Jacob Marley I knew."

"I am not the Jacob Marley you knew," the ghost replied. "I am Iacobus Marlius, the legendary Roman miser."

"I'm sorry," said Scrooge, "but I don't know much about Roman legends."

"Neither did I," Marlius said miserably. "If I had, I would have learned about Midas for a start."

Scrooge did know a little about Midas, for obvious reasons.

"I thought Midas was a Greek," he observed.

Marlius shrugged his shoulders. As he did so, the sickly green light coruscated so intensely that Scrooge felt nauseous as well as frightened.

"Greeks to us were like Romans are to you," he explained.

Scrooge thought for a moment. Something concerned him, and he soon identified what it was.

"Are you saying that you were condemned to be a ghost because you found some buried Greek coins?"

Marlius burst out laughing, but his laughter could not have had less merriment in it. If laughter could be coloured, it was sickly-green with sarcasm. What with that, and the even more virulent coruscations of the toga which the laughter set in motion, it was all that Scrooge could do to hold his chocolate cake down.

"I'm a ghost because I was a miser," he said. "They became so sick of me in Rome that they posted me to Britannia. It was either that or being handed over to the Vandals in exchange for the Emperor's third cousin once removed whom they were holding as a prisoner. So, I chose Britain. They asked me to set up a bank. Somebody thought Londinium had possibilities in that direction."

"And did you?" Scrooge inquired.

The toga blazed green and yellow and worse in all directions.

"Yes and no. I found a building, very expensive to rent for its size. I might say and I got a sign painted. Scrooge had lately taken an interest in art.

"What was on it?" Scrooge inquired with curiosity.

Marlius shrugged his shoulders. Scrooge wished that he hadn't.

"A bag of money. What else?"

"And what happened after that?" Scrooge asked.

Marlius took a deep breath. Scrooge was relieved the toga barely moved as he did so.

"There was this woman ..."

Scrooge resisted the temptation to say 'there usually is.' He now regretted that he had never married nor had children of his own, although there was a kindly widow ten doors up on the other side of his street!

He turned his attention to Marlius once more.

"She was called Bodicea," Marlius went on.

Scrooge's knowledge of history was even more deficient than his knowledge of art.

"A nice name." he said.

Marlius gave Scrooge a sideways look.

"She wasn't nice at all. She was one of your queens. Don't you know that?"

Scrooge shook his head.

"She led a revolt against us in East Anglia, and then marched towards London. They thought she might drive us out. That's why I buried these coins."

"And why didn't you dig them up again?" Scrooge asked.

"Because I was dead, that's why. I was a nominated hostage, you see. They, therefore, took me to the front line in the battle. If somebody important were captured, they could exchange me for them. And that's what they did."

"But why did they kill you?" Scrooge inquired.

"They weren't intending to kill me at first. But then they asked me what I did, and rather than tell them I was a miser, which I thought might turn them against me, I told them I was a banker, which I wasn't really, because I hadn't banked anything at that stage. And as soon as I told them I was a banker, they set on me. I've since found out on Spookipedia that the British have always had a particular hatred of bankers."

Scrooge had never heard of Spookipedia, and asked what it was.

"We have a thing called the internet," Marius explained. "Spookipedia is an encyclopaedia. You do a few things with your computer, as we call it, and you can look anything up. It's amazing what you learn. Did you know that there are some vampires who recoil from something called Marmite? And four out of five poltergeists self-harm at some stage? We also keep in touch; we can rattle our chains on a spectral network. It's called ClinkedIn. That's how I got in touch with Jacob Marley. We've become great friends; not that we've ever actually met."

Scrooge could not help asking what seemed to be an obvious question.

"How long would it take you to fly to see Marley in ... err ... if you don't object to the phrase, in person?"

Marlius thought for a moment.

"About two seconds. Three at the most."

Scrooge nodded.

And how fast is your, what do you call it, Internet connection?

The ghost considered.

"Shroudband speeds vary. Sometimes half a minute. Sometimes four or five minutes. I once had to try three times, and it took about ten. And sometimes it goes off altogether. Not that it bothers us. I mean, as you can see, this is quite a nice toga ..."

Scrooge shuddered.

"I try to keep up appearances. But if you'd seen the average spectre, not to mention the ghouls, you'd realise that going off is part of our way of life."

Scrooge remained silent because he did not know what to say. Then he thought of saying:

"Half a minute. Sometimes four or five?"

Marlius considered for a few seconds more than it would have taken him to fly to see Jacob Marley.

"Oh. "I see what you mean."

Scrooge thought of his former partner.

"Hasn't Marley said anything?"

The toga flickered stomach-churningly as Marlius shook his head.

"No."

"What about anybody else?"

Marlius frowned. Scrooge was glad to see that he had at least stopped shaking his head.

"To tell the truth, he's the only contact I keep in touch with. We seem to have a lot in common. Most of the others are only concerned with selling financial products.

I suppose it's my own fault for saying that I was a professional miser; didn't want to risk calling myself a banker again. They have these things called algorithms, whatever they are. But, as I said, it can be slow. I suppose I could change my provider. I've heard Haunt Haunt is quite good ..."

His voice tailed off.

"Why are you here?" Scrooge asked. "And if the idea doesn't distress you too much, why are you here now?"

Marlius quickly replied. "Here ... because my coins were here: Now ... because you found my last one, on your spade there."

"Do you want them?" Scrooge asked gently, maybe almost needlessly since he was sure the ghost's interest in them was anything but pecuniary.

The spirit shook his head.

Scrooge almost vomited and made a mental note not to ask any further questions requiring 'yes' or 'no' as an answer.

"What use is money to me? And in any case our coins are ten a penny."

Although that wasn't what the man in the British Museum had told him, Scrooge said nothing. He nowadays felt it was vulgar to talk about money, and that being the case, it would be even more vulgar to talk about money ... in relation to money.

"There must be Roman coins all over the place. Not in piles, I admit but individually; thousands and thousands of them. No civilisation in history, I tell you, has ever been, or ever will be, so careless with its small change. This could all be due to our relative lack of inventiveness. I'm sorry to admit it, but it's the truth. Spookipedia mentions this specifically."

Scrooge was puzzled by this, and gratified to see that Marlius appeared to have noticed, since he explained at once.

"Take the matter of numbers. Our numbers are, to put it kindly, all over the place."

Despite his general ignorance of history, Scrooge knew Roman numbers perfectly well, these being displayed on the clock in his office which he watched so closely before his repentance. This was not on his own account, but to see that Cratchit always arrived on time and never left early.

"Your numbers are still all over the place," he said. "Not only clocks, but public buildings."

Tombstones came to mind, but he thought it best not to mention them, and fell silent.

"I bet they're not in any place where you have to add them up," Marlius observed sarcastically. He took a deep breath. "And then there's the pointed arch. Pretty obvious, you might think. But we never invented that. And can you see something else we didn't invent?" He rustled his toga, which almost caused Scrooge to faint.

"Is there something you can't see?"

Apart from being unable to see the prospect of eating anything ever again, which he sensed was not the point, Scrooge could see nothing.

"Well," Marlius explained. "Can't you see that we never invented the pocket? That's why we were always dropping coins all over the place."

"I see," Scrooge said. "Can you possibly explain something else to me?"

"Well, if I can," Marlius said. "If I don't know the answer, I'll look it up on you-know-what and then I'll be back tomorrow."

"It's not that sort of question," Scrooge said hesitantly. "What I was wondering is ... why are you here, apart from the fact that I found your last coin. Were you trying to tell me that, so I won't waste time looking for any more? If so, that's very kind of you, but ..."

He didn't know how to finish.

Marlius did not seem to know how to start. Scrooge could see that there was something he wanted to say though. At length Marlius spoke.

"I was trying to help you, yes. It's not something I've ever done before. Jacob Marley recommended you. He thought that if I did something for you, then you might help me."

He hesitated for a moment.

"And him."

"Why didn't Jacob come?" Scrooge asked.

"He hasn't helped you since, well, you know. And that was some time ago. And he thinks his case is ... hopeless." Scrooge considered carefully.

"I take it there's nothing on Spookipedia."

"It's not that sort of knowledge. It's not numbers or arches or pockets."

Scrooge thought through the matter.

"I sometimes think I haven't changed," he said. "But your appearance has made me realise something. When I think I haven't changed, what I'm doing is haunting myself. Perhaps you're haunting yourselves too."

"But you're alive," Marlius said at once. "We're dead"

"No more dead than my old self. What's worrying you is that you're not dead. You both think that if you stop being misers, then you'll die. But you won't."

"What will happen to us?" Marius whispered, fearfully.

"I don't know," said Scrooge. "But whatever it is, you won't die. Can't you bring Jacob here?"

"All right," said Marlius, "I'll just text him."

"Fly to him yourself!" Scrooge commanded.

"Oh, yes," said Marlius. "I'd forgotten. Yes. Sorry."

Scrooge looked at the second hand of his watch. It was five and a half seconds later that the pair of them stood before him.

"Hello, Ebeneezer," said Jacob nervously.

"Hello, Jacob," said Scrooge, smiling warmly to reassure him.

"Ebeneezer has something to tell us both," Marlius explained.

Scrooge didn't realise that his words could have had such a fearful effect; the whole city seemed to resound with the most frantic knocking. Then there were anguished cries of something, and the sound of breaking glass. He closed his eyes in dread. Somebody was lifting the top half of his body, and he opened his eyes in terror to see his nephew.

Tears of relief were in his nephew's eyes.

"We thought you had ... you didn't arrive at our house, and there was no answer to the door! I had to borrow a ladder and break the window. Are you all right?"

"Yes," said Scrooge. "I must have overslept, that's all. You said I was expected ..."

"Of course you were expected!" his nephew gasped. "We told you. How could you not be expected? Where would we be without you?"

"At home," said Scrooge.

His nephew shook his head in disbelief.

"Where would we be without you ON CHRISTMAS DAY?"

Scrooge suddenly remembered.

"I'm so sorry," he said. "I must be getting older in my mind than I care to admit."

"There's nothing wrong with your mind," his nephew stated decisively. "You don't forget things, and you never oversleep. You've been up to something, Uncle. Now, what were you doing last night that made you forget Christmas?"

Scrooge hesitated.

"I did a couple of friends a good turn," he said. "At least I think I did. Hope I did anyway."

His nephew laughed.

"Well, Uncle, you keep telling me you aren't sure you have really changed. And now, on your own admission, you have forgotten it was

Christmas Day again; this time because you were so busy helping someone. If that isn't turning over a new leaf, I don't know what is. Now, we'd better hurry down without further ado. Poor Tom was beside himself; he felt certain you'd died."

"Why was that?" Scrooge asked.

"Well," his nephew began, "I'm sure you'll agree that Tom is a level-headed young lad."

Scrooge nodded.

"Down-to-earth."

Scrooge nodded again.

"Dibbing."

"Dibbing." Scrooge agreed.

"And, you know his bedroom window has a view of your garden."

"He waves to me sometimes," Scrooge confirmed.

His nephew cleared his throat.

"After dark last night, not long after he had left you, he saw a pair of angels rise up to heaven. At the time he thought they were bringing the great glad tidings to us all, but when you failed to arrive, he was certain they were carrying you away."

THE END

Stew
Mikaella Lock

He shoved her violently inside and the door slammed shut. Loudly. Abruptly. Metal scraped on metal like fingernails on a blackboard as the heavy-duty bolt slid and then clanked into place, sealing her in from the outside world ... away from her family; away from the living; away from salvation.

The room, dimly lit by a miserable little bulb hoisted high up on the ceiling, was filthy. The industrial tiles felt cold and sticky, smeared with God only knows what. The walls - just bare, crude brick - were rough and crumbling in places. And the smell, Christ, that smell. It reeked.

She lay there on the floor in a heap, her pretty, ecru blouse with the spring flower pattern ripped and crumpled, her black jeans soaked through from panic and fear.

Her mascara had stretched out inky fingers and daubed modern art around her puffy, watery eyes. She had somehow lost her shoes during the struggle, and her normally impeccably styled hair was in rats' tails, sticking to her neck and forehead framing her pale face like a Munch masterpiece.

Terrified, her breathing came in short, ragged gasps as she took in her immediate surroundings. Trapped-animal eyes darted about wildly as she struggled to see in the poor light. Too frightened to move even an inch, she could hear the thud of heavy footsteps receding. She would soon be alone. One small mercy at least.

***

"Mummy, Mummy, look! Look what I found for you! Look, pretty, pretty flowers!" The little girl clutched a ragged bunch of wilting pink campions and buttercups in one outstretched, chubby fist.

She skipped over to where her mother was sat reading a magazine, enjoying the rays of a summer sun.

"Oh, aren't they gorgeous? Thank you," her mother cooed. Smiling, she took the flowers and raised them to her nose, making a big show of smelling them.

"Where did you find all of those, Maisie?"

"At the garden bottom, at, at Mrs. Thoma - Thomassesses hedge. There's more, Mummy! Should I go and get more?"

Maisie pushed a strand of blonde hair behind her ear as she looked up excitedly at her mother, her little face beaming.

"I think we have enough to fill a vase, don't you agree? Besides, we don't want Mrs. Thomas getting upset, do we? She might think you're after her raspberries again, Maisie," her mother chuckled.

"Ok Mummy, I won't. Can I have a biscuit though? And a glass of juice? Please, Mummy?"

"Of course you can, my sweet. Come on then, let's go inside."

"Yay!"

Happily, Maisie skipped off towards the house, the sequined hem of her pink sundress shimmering in the warm, summer light. Placing the flowers down next to the magazine, her mother followed the small girl inside.

Watching the two figures disappearing into the house, Mason uncurled himself from where he had been hiding by his father's shed.

He had taken the small penknife from his father's wooden box and had been practising carving his name into an old log.

After the last thrashing his father had given him, his backside had been so sore he could barely sit down. He knew he shouldn't have taken the knife, but he didn't care.

Mason had learned a long time ago that crying or begging for the beatings to stop only made them worse. At least his father hadn't used the belt. Last time that happened, Mason thought that he might actually throw up and pass out.

He had felt so woozy and faint, and in so much pain. He had just wanted the floor to open up and swallow him whole as he had tried to stop himself from crying out as each blow fell.

He had bitten his lip so hard he had made it bleed as he tried not to scream.

His father had just sneered at him. Laughed at him. He could still see his stupid, ugly face, the mouth pulled back in a snarl, mocking him.

"You're no boy, no son of mine! Look at you! You're a pathetic little piece of shit!" his father had raged. "Get up off the floor, you snivelling little rat. You think it's ok to steal from the neighbours? I had that old bitch Thomas around again. Yeah, you know what you done, you piece of shit."

Thwack.

A child's stifled shriek.

Thwack.

His mother had looked on icily, her arms folded across her chest. His tear-filled eyes had searched her face, silently imploring her to do something – anything - to make the torment stop.

"Try to be quieter, Mason." she had hissed, turning her head away. "You'll upset Maisie."

***

She wasn't sure how long she had lain on the floor. It could have been a few minutes. It could have been a few hours. Fear plays odd tricks on the mind, and in this room, time had stopped.

It was impossible to tell if it was day or night. Her head felt stuffy, and her body was stiff. Her mouth was uncomfortably dry, her tongue claggy. She thought she could taste the metallic tang of blood but wasn't certain. She was still disoriented even though her eyes had adjusted to the gloomy confines.

Gritting her teeth, she sat up and looked around. Getting unsteadily to her feet, she felt a dull ache across her temple where he must have had hit her. She gingerly raised a hand to her head, wincing as fresh pain surged.

She fell against the wall behind her, her legs refusing to cooperate as she took long breaths, the brickwork scratching and snagging at the delicate material of her blouse.

The room wasn't large. It was blockish, roughly six metres by six she estimated.

Prison cell size.

The suspended bulb cast a vomit-yellow hue over the oddly elevated ceiling, highlighting all the stains and flecks that made it look as though someone had explosively sneezed up there. In one corner, she discerned a pile of old rags; colourless, dirtylooking, fly tip fabrics.

She stood up and shuffled over to the heap, nudging it with her foot. Not fly tip fabrics after all but a mish mash of grubby bed sheets, old fashioned and thin like the ones so easily found in the charity shops; the type of bed sheets people had died on.

Bending down, she gathered one up by the hem. She could see it was heavily soiled, smudged with a sickly brown colour. It looked like shit. Tentatively she sniffed it, grimacing. Not shit, but something else. Musty.

The odour was unpleasant like overripe cheese or fish just going over its sell-by-date. It seemed vaguely familiar, but she couldn't quite recall where she'd come across the smell before. Dropping the sheet back down, she shoved the pile with her foot, half expecting a swarm of cockroaches to come zigzagging out.

Nothing.Thank God.

To the left of the pile was a rusty bucket tipped over on its side.

There was something congealing within it. She couldn't tell what though.

She gave the bucket a one-fingered prod. Rolling around and rattling tinnily on the hard tiles, it fully exposed its maw.

"Eughhh!" she gagged.

That definitely was shit, no mistaking that stink. Repulsed, she kicked the bucket away, the clatter it made unnaturally loud in the confines of the small room.

What the hell is this place?

Turning, she peered at the wall opposite her. She could make out a series of aged, metal pegs, jutting out from the brickwork.She took a small step forward. Ah, no. Not pegs. They looked more like ... hooks. Rammed in at different heights, there was no real order to them and while they were undeniably corroded, they still seemed solid, and very strong. Were they some type of wall reinforcement? Some part of the architecture? Were they attachments for some sort of commercial shelving? It seemed very strange; the pegs – hooks - whatever they were, certainly appeared to serve no purpose.

So why are they there then?

She didn't want to think about it. In fact, she didn't want to think about it at all.

She quickly averted her eyes, a sickening realisation beginning to dawn.

You're stuck in here all alone; no one has a clue where you are... an unwelcome voice whispered in her head. *He's got you right where he wants you. In the dark. Scared. He's a lot bigger than you. He's a lot stronger than you ... there's nothing you can do. You're trapped in here ...*

"Oh, Jesus Christ, no!", she whimpered. She was supposed to sleep on that stinking heap, wasn't she? That revolting bucket was supposed to be her toilet. Fear's knell pealed and clanged inside her head as panic began rapidly bubbling up inside her again.

You're a prisoner, a captive! He can do what he likes to you ...

"Shut up! Shut up! Shut up!" she moaned, aghast. She screwed her eyes shut and willed the voice in her head to disappear. Her lips trembled as her wretched situation sank in like brass knuckles to the face. The voice was right. She didn't know where she was or what to do. Even worse, she had no idea who he was and what *he* was going to do.

The tears snaked hotly down her cheeks as she raised her balled up fists to her face, emitting a feral, keening sound as she did so. Slumping in defeat, she hugged her knees to her chest and let out a series of loud sobs, her soft, plump body shaking in despair.

How long was she going to have to stay in this godforsaken hole? What does he want? What the hell does all this mean?

Nothing good, of that she was now sure.

***

Once his mother and sister had walked up the steps to the house and vanished from sight, Mason quickly folded up and pocketed the penknife. It was on this same beautiful summer's day that he had woken up and felt something different.

There was a strange fire of defiance burning hotly inside him; he could feel it deep down in the pit of his stomach, searing and scalding. He had sensed it the moment he opened his eyes that morning, and he could still feel it now. It made him both exhilarated and frightened at the same time. And angry ... he was so incredibly angry.

Mason had seen Maisie picking the flowers and he had seen how his mother had fawned all over her when she'd presented them. His sister could never do anything wrong in his mother's eyes; he could never do anything right. It had always been that way.

He had always felt unloved and isolated as far back as he could remember. And it got so much worse when perfect princess Maisie had been born. There were no tender kisses on the forehead for Mason. Oh no. No cuddles, no sweet words of comfort ... only shouting, and yelling, and spiteful words, and pain. So much pain.

"I hate you," he muttered under his breath.

"I hate you so much."

Creeping out of the shadows, he sidled up to the table and stared at the flowers that had been left there. Glancing over his shoulder to check no one had noticed him he snatched them up and threw them to the ground before stamping on them repeatedly.

Breathing heavily, he stopped to admire his

work. The stems were twisted and torn, and the delicate blooms were crushed, pink and yellow petals scattered about the grass. Turning his attention to the magazine, he snorted in contempt. The model on the front looked a bit like his mother. Admittedly, it was a very vague resemblance, but a resemblance, nonetheless.

He withdrew the penknife from his pocket and flicked it open. With a sharp intake of breath, he raised it high above his head and stabbed downwards with all his might, ramming the wicked little blade into the model's face. He felt it pierce deep into the garden table with a satisfying '*thunk*', pinning the magazine in place through one of the model's beautiful, jade-green eyes.

Mason snickered as he retrieved the knife, tugging doggedly on its handle to free it from the wood. Tonight, he was determined he was not going to cry. He wouldn't even whimper!

When that hiding came - and he knew it would come - he would force himself to stay silent. It would be hard he knew, but he was determined. It would be worth it just to see their faces.

His father, his face florid and breath stinking of beer, would do what he normally did; and his mother would do what she normally did; and they'd expect Mason to do what he normally did.

Cower like a baby and try not to squeal too loud. Well, guess what… No more! Things are going to be very, very different from now on, he thought resolutely.

"Who's crying now pig turds? Cos' it won't be me, fuckers!" He spewed the swear words out, enjoying hearing them fall recklessly and audibly from his mouth. He giggled rebelliously to himself as he ran off back towards the shed.

For the first time in his miserable, young life, Mason felt in complete control.

*****

Tightly huddled up, she had been crying for a long time. Her wracking sobs had eventually given way to soft whimpers, which had finally petered out to an occasional, raspy hiccup.

A strange, self - imposed catatonia had then followed as she sank deep into herself with angst. But she was stirring now.

The tears had dried, leaving her face sore and red, and her cheeks flushed and hot. Unappeased, the primordial instinct of fight or flight was proving more of a hindrance than an evolutionary benefit. There was nothing to fight and no means of running away.

She was struggling to shake off the mental fuzziness of overwhelming emotion, and rushing cortisol had made her limbs feel heavy and leaden.

Think! She urged herself. *You've got to start thinking if you're going to get out of this.*

Steeling her resolve, she sniffed wetly, aggressively rubbing under her nose with her sleeve. She returned to the moment she had been abducted, taking the jigsaw-piece memories one by one, attempting to construct something coherent, something understandable.

If she could find a rationale, a bit of logic, she

might be able to use that information to her advantage. Maybe even escape.

***

Upstairs, he was in the kitchen whistling along to Taylor Swift.

The lyrics echoed melodically. *'So why can't you see',*

A clatter of utensils as he dug about in the cupboard. More strident whistling.

'All this time, how could you not know…'

A cough, hawking something viscous and green into the sink.

'…You belong with me. You belong with me'.

Chop, slice. Chop, slice. Chop, slice.

Smirking now.

Muttering, acapella.

"This fat pig belongs to me."

He tossed onions into a sizzling pan.

***

It was Tuesday when he took her. She remembered she had finished work early and had met up with Chloe and Jess at The Zone. They'd had a few drinks, non-alcoholic for her because she was driving, and ate a few snacks together; chatted about Chloe's new role in marketing. It had still been bright when she left.

What time had she made a move? Around 7-ish?
She'd planned to nip into the local supermarket to pick up butter and milk and other bits; all the stuff

she'd run low on. Oh, and that posh cheese and herbs she needed to try out; the new dish Jess had been going on about.

Ok ... boring, mundane, routine.

It had, however, been fabulously hazy that evening she recollected. Far too balmy and bright to waste trudging supermarket aisles so she had decided to go to the Memorial Gardens and Park to sit by the lake instead. She had parked up and paid at the Pay & Display.

Good! The ticket would have expired. Someone will notice my car hasn't moved, surely? My driver's licence is in my handbag, they'll be able to ID me as the owner'.

She'd left her bag in the foot-well, passenger side, under the blanket like usual. Just took her phone ...

My phone!

With a gasp, she frantically patted her jeans.

Don't be an idiot ... he's not going to leave you with a phone, is he?

The voice in her head chided. *Get back to thinking with your brain and not your ass.*

"Dammit!" she shouted aloud.
Fine, I'm an idiot. Let me get back to it! She mentally remonstrated with herself. *Right, so*

handbag under the blanket, took my phone…

She had been strolling to the quiet spot where she could lie back on the grass and listen to the sounds of the insects buzzing and birds chirping.

Her secret, magical spot; idyllic and peaceful; undisturbed by yelling kids, barking dogs or gossiping mothers. One of the very few places she knew close by where she could sit all by herself, and completely switch off from the world if she chose to. Only she had never made it. That's when he attacked her. She had just stepped off the footpath and had been meandering through the trees…then blackness.

She touched her sore temple:

Bastard. He must have hit me and knocked me out. Did he follow me or was he already there just waiting for someone to walk past?

She remembered coming to in the boot of a car, her hands and feet bound and her body gently rolling in time with the vehicle's momentum.

There had been a rough cloth in her mouth preventing her from screaming. It had tasted awful and had made her gag. She had been terrified she would be sick and end up choking on her own vomit.

She hadn't been able to see very much, just the dark fluff of the boot lining and the blurry outlines of a few empty cartons; probably old screen wash bottles.

Whatever he had tied her wrists with had been gnawing sharply into her skin. She could hear the thrum of traffic outside, feel the vibration of the car's engine when it idled.

Idled.

She had heard the drone of voices then. People ... lots of them. He had been at traffic lights. The awareness that she was so close to rescue yet simultaneously so far had been bitterly absurd, she recalled.

Unable to raise the alarm with either her voice or her fists, she had resorted to flopping her body about seal-like in the hope she could make a thump loud enough to draw attention. It had been woefully ineffective, but he must have noticed because he had turned the music on.

Ariana Grande or some other crappy pop shit.

The car moved with alacrity after that. The corners were turned a little more urgently ,the engine pitch was higher, and the rolling of her body in the dark confines of the boot had been a little less forgiving. No more idling or drone of voices, no more stops and starts. He had clearly left the town and was driving on open road.

He was hardly going to murder you in front of a crowd, was he? Need to go somewhere private, out of the way for that.

She winced, cursing the logic of her inner voice. It must have been a good road, well-asphalted, as there had been no bumps or tight turns, no major deceleration or stopping for lights, and no pumping of brakes. The journey had continued at pace.

Must have been on that road for a good hour. It would have been well past the home time rush so he would have had an easy cruise. He had to have been on either an A-road or a motorway; impossible to know which though. How long had she been unconscious for?

A significant slowing of the car as it navigated sharper corners, and more twists and turns, signalled that he had exited whichever main thoroughfare he'd been on.

She had heard the switch in gears as the car went uphill and downhill; felt the engine pull on the incline and push off the decline.

It had been uncomfortable, but bearable - a complete contrast to the final stretch of her involuntary road trip.

That had been horrendous ... but at least he had turned the music off. She had been jolted and knocked about as the car had swayed from side to side, presumably to avoid potholes and debris. Evidently there were too many to miss as jarring clunks and crunches had shaken her bones and rattled her teeth over and over. She had heard the splash of puddles as the tyres rumbled through them, and the shrill creaking of the suspension as he negotiated a path clearly better suited to a rugged and reliable 4x4.

People don't take cars up tracks like that - not sane ones anyway. Dirt tracks don't lead anywhere, just old farms or fields. It's remote, definitely ...

It had felt like an eternity before the car had come to a stop. The wrist bindings had bitten deeper and deeper, and she'd been mouthing at the coarse gag pushing at its threads with her tongue trying in vain to loosen it, until it was sodden with saliva.

The paresthesia in her lower legs had become close to intolerable, so much so she was positive she would be unable to walk.

She had heard the scrunch of wheels on gravel, the crank of a handbrake and felt the rocking motion as he had climbed out, slamming the car door.

A fresh wave of trepidation had flooded over her as she listened to his footsteps, heavy and ominous, drawing level with the boot.

She had hardly dared to breathe when he spoke, his voice husky in timbre.

'I'm only telling you this once. Don't do anything stupid and don't try anything stupid', he had warned.

Some clicking noises, a squeak, and the boot had sprung open. She had found herself squinting up at the dazzling, synthetic light of a very bright head torch and the hulking silhouette of a man looming menacingly over her.

He had stared down at her silently for an agonisingly long period of time. It had made her skin crawl, and she had instinctively recognised his instability and unpredictability.

'*If you do, I'll cut your fucking eyes out'*, he had added.

*** *** ***

Mason wasn't sure how he was going to do it yet; he hadn't thought that far ahead. But what he did know was Maisie had to disappear ... and his father too. That would upset his mother.

She would cry and wail, and shriek and whine, and then cry and wail some more. How he craved to see her upset and distressed for once; see the cold-hearted bitch crack.

Mason of course couldn't have known, but he had been unplanned. It was as a result of an ill-conceived and drunken one-night stand that his mother had fallen pregnant with him.

Fearing the shame and embarrassment of her folly, she had tearfully confided in a close family friend who had advised passing the boy off as her husband's.

'*There's no need for him to know. It was a one-off, right?*'

Cooing and patting and consoling, the friend convinced her that there was no need to suspect that the happy, chubby little boy was anyone else's.

'*The chances of him being a stranger's child are so slim after all - what are the odds?*' she had soothed. '*It's just the timing. The pregnancy just happens to coincide with what you did that night.*

Try to forget about it. Why risk your marriage and your happiness on a 'what if'?'

Mason's naïve and frightened young mother had gratefully agreed.

But he had found out, and he had been furious when he did. The indiscretion had come to light following a particularly heated argument with the same close family friend who had advised that Mason's uncertain origins remain a secret.

The truth had been spat out loudly and vindictively. A hushed silence had followed before a swift, red-faced retraction, but it was too late. The damage had been done. With Mason's biological parentage in question, the boy had become the excuse for every quarrel, every fight, every slanging match. He was the fuse that lit the inferno ... and he was loathed for it.

As he grew, he did not develop any of his father's features. His hair was dark like his mothers, but he was becoming a tall, well-built young lad; nothing like his sinewy, short-statured father. From the very beginning his father had made it clear he wanted nothing to do with his son.

It was with the remarkable resilience only a child can possess that little Mason learned to adapt and cope: to deflect his father's malice and heartlessness; to accept and repress what he felt when his father hurt him.

His mother was a different kettle of fish. Her approach towards her son was cold, unflinching indifference. It had started with shoves at first. He would toddle to her with outstretched arms, and she would push him roughly away. She soon stopped holding him entirely. She never wiped away his tears or cuddled him. She never comforted him when he was poorly or sad. Wouldn't put a plaster on his knee or put his drawings on the fridge.

He had never experienced the tender kisses of a loving mother or had a bedtime story read to him. She fed him and cleaned him adequately enough, made sure he was educated and provided for him, but that was only to keep up appearances. How shameful it would be to have a dirty, scruffy, illiterate child after all.

Then Maisie had come along. Pure and untainted Maisie. His mother loved her unconditionally. Showered the baby girl with all the affection and compassion she should have also shown her young son. Even his father had demonstrated a softer side, bouncing the little girl on his knee and laughing at her little gurgles and squeaks.

He never raised a fist to Maisie, even when she misbehaved. Unlike Mason. He had smiled on cue; had always tried to be on his very best behaviour; and systematically hid his bruises under colourful, long-sleeved t-shirts with robots and dinosaurs printed on them.

On a rare day out as a family, a casual observer might look over and smile fondly at the spirited little girl, the quiet little boy and two content-looking parents eating ice-creams. A more perceptive observer might look over and notice that the only one not eating an ice-cream was the quiet little boy who didn't fidget and laugh quite as loud as his sister.

They might notice that pensive little boy staring into space, wishing he too could eat an ice-cream. This was a little boy who even though he was with his family in a bustling café, surrounded by so many happy, jovial people, knew profoundly within his soul that he was completely and utterly alone.

***

She was on her feet, her socks clinging tackily underfoot as she padded across to the door she had been bundled so unceremoniously through.

It was wooden and sturdy with peeling paintwork in a colour that had long faded. She ran her fingers over it, feeling the thin, crispy paint shards coming away at her touch. It was firmly closed and clearly very secure.

There was no friendly little brass knob she could turn; no shiny silver handle she could flip up and down. Nor was there any glimmer of light coming from underneath it or emanating from the jambs. It must be locked from the outside, she reasoned.

She got down on all fours and pressed her face to the floor, flinching as her skin connected with the grubby tiles. The space beyond was forebodingly dark. No draughts. She sat up on her knees, rubbing her palms on her jeans.

You were dragged down those steps before he flung you in here. You must be in a cellar or a basement. You know you're way out somewhere in the sticks. It's doubtful anyone would hear you through those thick walls ... and there is no way you are opening that door. No point screaming for help.

She stood up and began pacing around the room. Returning to the pile of rags, she picked through them in turn, shaking each one out hoping to find a clue, no matter how small, that could provide some insight as to what might lie in store for her.

Forewarned is forearmed. Let's be realistic. You'd probably be dead already if he didn't have plans for you. He's going to keep you alive for a little while at least. Why else would there be a bucket to shit in and rags to lie on?

Nothing! Sighing, she dropped the last stained rag.

Ok, ok. Don't give up. Let's try this again from a different angle.

Working methodically, she traced the boundaries of the room searching for anything that might help her escape: a nook between the stones; a loose floor tile; she even righted that ungodly bucket again and checked inside it.

Nothing. Still vile.

She wrinkled her nose in disdain. Squatting down, she fumbled about in all the shadowy recesses where something may have fallen and was now lying concealed in the murk. Her knees complaining loudly, she made her way awkwardly around the room shuffling on the balls of her feet, forensically searching on the ground with her hands.

Must eliminate all possibilities, no matter how puke-inducing that elimination is.

Her hand brushed against something furry ... and rigid. She hesitantly picked it up with her fingertips, feeling it peel off the floor.

What is that?

Delicate bones protruded from a straggly pelt and the skin of the skull had withered exposing the jaw, rictus-like; a small animal, long dead given its crispy, flat appearance.

"Oh, ugghh, no!" she yelped.

Quickly hurling it away, she frenziedly rubbed her hands on the material of her blouse, trying to wipe away the feel of matted fur. Was that small carcass responsible for the stink in the room? She wondered.

No, impossible.

All the animal's soft parts had already rotted away. And there had been no whiff of active decay to it. It had been too dry, too shrivelled, just a slight mustiness to it.

Like that stained sheet you sniffed.
Fuck.

The stench in the room was different though. The putridness lingered in the air as if it was emanating from the walls themselves. It made the whole room smell … rotten.

Like a fresher dead animal … a bloated dead animal rotting wetly and slimily …

When she was a child, she had been on a camping holiday to Spain with her cousins. The adults had been busy preparing a barbeque, and the children had slipped off to explore the lake nearby.

They'd been playing at the water's edge, skimming stones and looking for tadpoles in the reeds. As they'd waded further in, they noticed a strange odour.

"Ewwww! Holly, did you fart?" she'd asked, holding her nose.

"No! I thought it was Caroline!" Holly had denied indignantly.

"What's that smell then? It stinks!"

The girls had searched for the source, and it hadn't taken long to find it. A dead rabbit was snagged up in the vegetation, the swollen body floating and bobbing in the water. Its chestnut brown fur was missing in patches, exposing the greyish-blue skin beneath. Its bulging, sightless eyes fixed the girls in a milky stare as they approached it.

The stench had been too pungent to get right up to it, but they could see the pulsating mass of maggots that feasted on the decaying flesh. The children had stared at it for a long while, their natural curiosity getting the better of them. They'd dared each other to see who could get closest to it without gagging.

Hands over their noses and mouths, and trying not to inhale too deeply, they had poked the body with long sticks, watching as fat, white maggots dropped into the water and sunk beneath the surface.

"It smells like Granddad Joe's feet!" Caroline had exclaimed, and they'd all tittered in amusement.

"No, I think it smells like Miss Tyman's breath," Holly had returned.

"Ugghh!" They'd chorused in unison.

"It's so gross, I've never seen a dead thing before, have you?" she had asked her cousins.

"No, not a big dead thing like that. Only the goldfish when they die. Daddy flushes them down the toilet," Caroline had explained. "They don't smell at all though."

Double fuck.

***

He had relished seeing her gawk blindly up at him when he had opened the boot, delighted to see the flicker of terror in her eyes when he'd threatened to cut them out.

She hadn't made a sound, even when he'd roughly lugged her out of the boot and dumped her face down in the gravel. Bending to grab her hair and yank her head back, he knew the pressure on her lower back must have been excruciating when he dug his knee into it.

He was pretty convinced she had pissed herself at that point, probably thinking he was going to slice her neck. A tempting prospect. But, instead, he had slipped the sack over her head, swiftly securing it in place, before hoisting her to her feet.

All trussed up and disoriented, she had slumped and sagged against him. He had needed to prop her up before tossing her over his broad shoulder and heading off up the driveway and across the yard.

The sack over the head was always a bit of fun. Sensory deprivation. One of those little touches that elicited such different responses. Some screeched and wailed. Some swore and cursed at him. Others remained silent, frozen in the headlights like she had. But they all cracked in the end. It was simply a matter of time and technique.

He wondered how she'd feel about her meal. He'd collected some decent roadkill this time and the snap traps had yielded a few pickings including a good-sized rat.

He was excited to give her the cat though. It had been pancaked and scooping it up into a bag had been a pain.

She'd be down there for a while until he was ready for her. He'd already marked an X on the calendar commemorating her abduction. Would he get to mark a second X commemorating her first feed?

He never cooked anything he chucked down the hole, it got lobbed in as it was. Raw, decaying, diseased. It didn't matter, pigs ate anything and everything.

Besides, if she wouldn't eat voluntarily, then

he'd just blend it all up and force it down her gullet as he usually did.

He smirked.

Music was still playing in the kitchen.

'You are the one that I want, you are the one I want, ooh, ooh, ohh, honey...'

He opened the cupboard and retrieved a large, heavy stew pot. Placing it on the hob, he filled it with water and set it to boil. The vegetables, peeled and cubed, were ready to simmer. A thick slab of red meat joined the onions sizzling away in the pan. Got to sear in the flavour before chopping it up; it tastes so much better that way.

***

The time Mason had spent nurturing and developing his ideas, his carefully crafted plans, thinking about the tableaux, the scenarios, the outcomes ... it all went completely out the window. There was no need for a plan. Not when the perfect opportunity presented itself on a scintillating silver platter.

At approximately quarter past five on a Friday afternoon in mid-July, the objects of his ruminations were smack dab where he needed them to be. This was a sign. Bored of flicking through the same, stupid book he'd read a million times, he had wandered over to his bedroom window to see if there were any insects he could crush between the mould-spotted net curtains and the glass.

That's when he had seen them: Maisie gesticulating erratically in that adorable way five-year olds do; and his father standing rigid and focused, his hands working something on the bench, pausing every now and again to nod in agreement with whatever Maisie was blathering about.

It was destiny, no doubt about it. Mason could feel the butterflies in his stomach, the over-emphasis of the gulp when he swallowed.

He could hardly believe his luck; Maisie and his father in the shed together - (*together!*) - his mother out around old Mrs. Shelt's place doing who-cares-what. The collision of fates was simply beautiful in its perfection. But he had to act fast.

Snatching up his hoodie from the bed, Mason hastily shrugged it on and rushed out of the bedroom. Hurtling down the stairs, he leapt off the remaining three and headed straight for the kitchen.

He tugged the yellow painted drawer under the sink forcefully open, almost pulling it off its runners. The contents clinking and rattling, his hands shaky with adrenaline, he searched frantically for the box he knew his mother kept in there.

He found it wedged right at the back. Triumphantly he scooped it up and tucked it into his hoodie. He then sprinted to the hallway to hastily put his trainers on. Laced up, his heart pounding in his chest, he slipped out the front door. But not before grabbing the spare set of keys hanging on the little hook next to the side jamb.

Slinking weasel-like around the side of the

house, Mason was careful not to step on anything that might make a sound and alert the *'targets'*.

'Targets'. I like that, he sniffed.

He had to be cautious. Although the shed was towards the bottom of the garden, he would still be momentarily in view before he could get to the garage.

If Maisie spotted him, she would be sure to open her big gob and the game would be up. Glancing over his shoulder, he could see they still had their backs turned to him.

Yes! So far so good.

He briskly walked the short distance from the top of garden to the wrought iron gate nestled in the dense laurel hedging. Unlatching it, he passed through and hurriedly made his way up the short, steep path, towards the garage.

Once at the blue, up-and-over, canopy door, Mason took the keys out of his pocket, bent down and deftly unlocked it, lifting the door just enough so he could squeeze under it.

If it goes up any higher it might make that weird, squealing sound, and then his father, that turd, would come running, Mason had thought.

Slipping silently inside, he noticed his adrenaline-induced shaking had subsided and his breathing had calmed. In fact he felt reasonably in control now, even with the butterflies still flipping and flitting inside him. It was an unusual sensation, but he found it incredibly gratifying.

Blinking as his eyes adapted to the dark interior, he spotted the green jerry cans in the far corner next to the lawnmower. With the dust motes swirling around his head, he picked a can up in each hand and tested their weight. They both sloshed as he shook them.

Bingo!

***

She knew she was in deep shit.

The stained rags, crap in a bucket ... there's no way in hell he's new to this. You're not the first in here, no way. Who knows what the fuck he's planning? You need to get out and you need to get out fast.

With renewed vigour, she closely examined the nasty looking hooks dotted randomly around the room, jiggling each one hoping she could pry it out to use as a weapon.

They were all robust and sturdy though. She'd already scoured the room for clues from floor to eye-level and that had proven fruitless.

Well, if he thought you had any chance of escape, he wouldn't have untied you or taken that hood off, would he? He obviously knows you can't get out. He's probably watching you through one of those see in the dark cameras right now ... laughing at you scrabbling about in the dirt trying to save your skin.

She gasped, snapping her head back and looked up at the high ceiling, studying it carefully.

What am I looking for? A tiny, blinking red light? Is it really like the movies?

No tell-tale signs of any cameras - not that she could see anyway. No cobwebs, no flies or moths throwing themselves suicidally against the lightbulb. Just rows of uniform, untextured and muck-covered panels.

Hang on...

There *was* something up there after all. She narrowed her eyes, trying to get a better look. Was that some form of metal fastening in the corner? Another hook?

No, too flat

But it was hard to tell exactly. She needed to get closer.

She retrieved the bucket and, ignoring its contents, upturned it next to the wall. Clambering onto it, she stood precariously on tip toe, trying not to lose her balance, and hoping the bucket wouldn't give way underneath her.

Gritting her teeth, she placed her right foot on the lowest hook she could find and stretched out her right hand reaching for the hook above her head.

Clutching it, she hauled herself up, raising her

left foot up onto the next closest protrusion, and stretching out with the other hand, seeking purchase on the hook there. Cling, pull and up. Repeat. Cling, pull and up.Repeat.
Just like rock-climbing.

She had made good progress and had managed to get some decent distance between her feet and the floor. Star-fished against the wall, she licked her lips, negotiating her next move, eyeing up suitable hooks, her body straining with effort as she gripped on tightly. That's when she heard a shuffling sound above her head. She looked up, curiously.

A small trapdoor had swung opened directly above her; the fastening she had seen a hinge. Its flap smacked against the wall revealing a narrow hole in the ceiling.

"Hey!" she shouted. "Hey, what do ..."

She didn't have time to finish her sentence. A rain of dead animals and offal slopped onto her face, knocking her off the wall.

She tumbled backwards onto the floor, cracking the back of her head, the wind completely knocked out of her. Stunned, and laying supine with the strong metallic smell of blood in her nostrils, she could see that the trapdoor had already been closed.

***

It had been simpler than he thought it would be. Maisie and his father had been so engrossed in whatever they were doing, they had been completely unaware as Mason had circuited the shed, emptying the jerry cans as he did so.

He'd kicked the shed door closed and snapped the large, shiny padlock back in place, ignoring his father's startled shout of surprise. Taking the box out of his hoodie pocket and lighting the match had been so easy.

Time had slowed in that moment: he'd heard the scratch of the match head on rough, red phosphorous; smelled the sharp whiff of sulphur as the tiny flame ignited, so small yet so powerful.

He had watched it for a moment, appreciating the gentle yellow flicker as it steadily devoured the thin strip of wood he held in his fingertips. Then, without a second thought Mason had casually flicked it down into the saturated grass around the shed door.

***

CONVERSATION BETWEEN PARAMEDIC AARON TURNBALL AND FIREFIGHTER JOHN BALDE, STAG AND BUGLE PUB, AT 22.30, 19JULY 2002.

Paramedic: "I've never seen anything like it, mate, scared the shit out of me if I'm honest."

Firefighter: "It's shocking, isn't it? There was accelerant all around the place, went up in a fucking inferno, boom, just like that. He was lucky the backdraft blew him clear in all fairness. He could have lit up too, he stank of petrol, man."

Paramedic: "He was fine, just superficial burns and a few cuts and bruises, nothing major. Still had to transport him though obviously. He was as excited as when he was telling me how it went 'whoomph', you know, when he threw the match. He was saying how he was listening to them, heard them screaming and that ... said they sounded like squealing pigs. Jesus"

Firefighter: "God, that's fucked up. There's something really fucking wrong with the boy. Did you see him smiling though? Baz said he was acting really odd ... like ... not what you'd expect from a young lad, you know?"

Paramedic: "Yeah, I did. Kerry was dressing his burns in the back of the wagon. I kid you not, he was there going '*ahhhh, oink oink, ahhhhoink oink,* just grinning from ear to ear. He couldn't take his eyes off that fucking fire. He wanted to see the bodies, kept asking me what they looked like. Fucked me right up that did, sent shivers down my spine."

Firefighter: "Really? He wanted to see the bodies? Holy ... and what? You mean he was like ... actually like pretend screaming? Maybe it was shock or something?"

Paramedic: "Yep. Smiling and fake screaming like he was mimicking the sounds they'd made when they were burning. And nah, mate, it wasn't shock - definitely not. The kid's a nutcase, like big time nutcase. After today, people are going to need some serious fucking therapy, mate, I tell you. Hell, I think *even I* might need therapy."

Firefighter: "Holy shit, man, that's onna whole 'nother level of crazy. The mother was a state though, wasn't she? Hardly surprising..."

Paramedic: "Yeah, had to get benzos into her sharpish."

Firefighter: "Fuuuuuuck. You up for another round, mate?"

Paramedic: "Yep, sure thing. I'll get 'em in. Same again mate?"

NEWSPAPER ARTICLE AS REPORTED BY KAREN
SHINE FOR THE DAILYPOST.

Alone

LOCAL COMMUNITY IN SHOCK AS FATHER AND DAUGHTER PERISH IN FIRE SET BY ELEVEN-YEAR-OLD SON.

Did YOU witness the blaze? Email
karen.shine@dailypost.co.uk
Published:8.30, 20 July 2002

The people of Aldershot were in shock yesterday after father of two, Kameron Pierce, and his five-year old daughter were tragically killed in a blaze allegedly set by Mr. Pierce's eleven-year-old son.

Emergency services were called to a residence in Ash Vale on Friday in response to reports that two individuals had been trapped in a garden shed that had 'gone up like a bonfire'.

Appalled residents told Daily Post how they had seen 'loads of smoke' and that 'all hell broke loose' when they realised 'a man and his little girl' were trapped inside. One person who preferred not to be named said: 'I will never, ever forget it. I could hear loud screaming, such horrific screaming. I ran outside to see what was going on.

There were a lot of people already in the street. Someone said there's a little girl and her dad trapped in there. I could see the fire. It was just awful.'

Dean Callington, who lives a couple of houses down from the Pierce family, said: 'I saw the family quite regularly, they seemed lovely. I just can't believe this has happened. Me and three other guys tried to get them out before the fire brigade got there, but it was impossible. There was no way of getting close, it was just too hot'.

Another witness who also wished to remain anonymous said: 'There were petrol cans in the garden. The young boy did it people have been saying. I don't think that's true though. It was horrendous, the wife had to be sedated'.

Officers have now cordoned off the area and forensic teams have been in attendance.

When asked to comment, Hampshire Police said: 'emergency services responded at around 17.35 on Friday afternoon to multiple calls that a man and his daughter were trapped in a garden shed on fire in Ash Vale, GU12. Fire crews were quick to bring the fire under control, but two people have sadly lost their lives. There is reason to believe the cause of the fire is arson. Our enquiries are ongoing'.

Mr. Pierce's son, who cannot be named for legal reasons, was found by onlookers in the garden of the Pierce family's home with minor burns. Mr. Pierce's wife, Lynette, 30, who had been over at a friend's house at the time of the incident, was described as 'inconsolable' by witnesses. Both mother and son were taken to Frimley Park Hospital for assessment.

Unfortunately, ambulance crews pronounced Kameron Pierce, 35, and daughter Maisie, 5, dead on the scene.

PSYCHOLOGICAL PROFILING REPORT, EXTRACT:
SECTION III. (1A), P12.ASSIGNED EXPERT:
CONSULTANT PSYCHOLOGIST MARTIN KEPPLER,
MSC, DCLINPSY, AFBPSS, LL.M.
CONFIDENTIAL – NOT FOR DISSEMINATION
PATIENT NUMBER: 00266634
CASE REPORT: CHILD X
DATE: 13TH OF AUGUST 2002.

A clear indicator of empathy dysfunction, the dehumanisation of father and sibling as '*targets*' aligns with core, secondary psychopathic characteristics and a dissociative pathway concomitant to callous-unemotional (CU) youth. Moreover, Child X exhibits co-morbid schizotypal traits and conduct disorder markers. Exposure to perpetuated and severe physical maltreatment within the family unit; chronic verbal hostility and humiliation by primary caregivers; and sustained neglect and deprivation habitually result in physical and / or emotional ontogenetic stunting. The chronicity of Child X's environmental adversity, the patricide and pedicide by arson committed by

Child X, and Child X's past and current semiology, warrant an immediate intervention. This should entail close monitoring within a high security, clinical setting, 24-hour supervision, anda rigorous and dynamic treatment regimen.

Empirically, the link between schizotypal behaviours, specifically aggression, and psychopathy has been well documented in adults. However, clinicians must exercise caution as the same construct in the case of pre-adolescents may only suffice in the short-term vis-à-vis risk appraisal and management. This is due to the significant developmental changes experienced by this demographic. Long-term clinical decision-making and management of Child X, therefore, should not focus solely on the psychopathy trifecta as a basis for treatment if a satisfactory prognosis and subsequent placement with alternative care givers are to be attained.

The WISC-V score of 152 places Child X in the highly gifted category...'

***

She was suspended from the ceiling by her feet, paracord wrapped in a thick bundle around her ankles. Fastened just above the trapdoor and invisible from below, a block and tackle pulley ensured an easy hoist and a secure, non-slip hold. Her arms were splayed out Christ-like, held in position by more bindings wound tightly around a couple of wall hooks.

In agonising discomfort, the inversion was causing an immense pressure build-up behind her eyes and inside her head.

She felt nauseous and faint. Like a bungee jumper with nowhere to go, she hung high above the tiles completely helpless.

"Different pegs for different pigs," his deep voice suddenly bellowed.

"You're all different sizes and shapes, although

I was always told not to play with my food ... really, quite strongly."

He hammered the last three words out venomously.

"Did you know that it's a common misconception, when the throat is cut, the blood comes fountaining out, shooting up to the sky. There's really not a massive spurt; no stupendous, crimson red geyser. That's actually incredibly rare. The initial ... jet ... shall we call it ... normally fizzles out around the seven-to-eight-inch mark."

She heard his footsteps ringing as he approached her; could see the tops of his shoes as he stopped, standing in front of her, his face level with the back of her head.

"It's misrepresented in the movies all the time," he continued, "cinematic effect!"

He puffed out his cheeks, before forcefully releasing the air with a loud 'pwwhhhh' as he sighed fatalistically.

"I personally find it incredibly frustrating. It ruins the whole experience for me.

Mind you, in your case dangling upside down as you are, it would be more of a waterfall, wouldn't it?"

He gave her tethered body a push.

She shrieked piercingly at his touch, her body shaking and jiggling as she recoiled.

"Oh my God, you're sick, you really are sick," she wailed wretchedly.

"You need help. Keep away from me! Please, I'm begging you, just leave me alone!"

"In reality, it's a series of small squirts that gradually ebb to a trickle and then nothing as the heart finally stops pumping," he stated impassively, ignoring her.

"The splashes and flicks all over the ceiling and in those hard-to-reach places in this room, the ones I couldn't be bothered to slosh down, those are cast-off from the blade; I can get a little carried away sometimes. Isn't that fascinating?"

He grabbed a fistful of her hair and wrenched, pulling her head up so he was eye-to-eye with her. She'd hated herself for thinking it, but his face was attractive - handsome even - yet, in that moment, she saw nothing behind his eyes except sinister darkness and an unfathomable callousness, terrifying in its rawness; a tumbleweed of a soul, blackened and devoid of emotion. She knew he was lost ... and so was she.

"Get the fuck away from me! Don't touch me!" She screamed at him, her spittle stippling his face.

She desperately tried to shy away, her body arcing like a bow. He released his grip on her hair, and she struggled violently against her restraints hearing the pulley squeak and rattle above her, feeling the scratching friction of the cords on her skin.

"Please, don't do it! Please don't! Please don't!" she implored over and over, lurching her body furiously from side to side, her eyes searching for an escape. As she twisted and turned, she caught glimpses of a narrow, honed blade held loosely in his hand; she saw a flash of blue plastic; saw the dark material of a pair of trousers…

He stepped back and watched as she struggled, fighting against the restraints, gasping and shrieking, snot and tears spattering onto the tiles;

he watched as she struggled and as she growled and whined primaevally, her body feebly jerking, growing weaker and weaker; and he watched until she could struggle and speak no more. Completely exhausted, her body went limp. It was over; she knew it and she knew he knew it. She closed her eyes.

He grinned broadly, savouring the moment before delivering his pièce de résistance.

"A *small* adult, human body … hmmm, let's say 66 kilos … yields roughly 55.3kg of potentially edible parts, leaving me around 18% to dispose of."

He paused, tapping his nose thoughtfully.

"Making bone stock is just *so* time-consuming though, especially when Knorr do such prettily packaged cubes, so we can knock off probably a further 8kg by taking the skeleton out of the equation.

That leaves us with 47.3kg of edible parts, and 33% to dispose of. Ah, but almost three kilos of you will be on the floor after I slit your throat - that means your blood by the way if you're struggling to keep up. I know it must be difficult taking all this in whilst you're hanging upside down."

He gently stroked her cheek whilst pulling a glum face in commiseration.

"And yes, I know, I know, there are approximately 5.5 litres of blood which would make it 5.5kgs on the floor … *but* it's impossible to drain it all. Capillaries, organs, etcetera, etcetera - they retain a percentage, you see.

So, taking that retention into account and presuming my calculations are correct - which they are - we would be left with, let's see…" He made a show of counting on his fingers exaggeratedly.

"44.3kg of edible parts which gives us 39 - 40% to chuck away. But that's what this barrel is for."

He rapped on the blue plastic with his knuckles.

"Now, I know a gentleman should never ask the question, but just to confirm, how much do you weigh?"

***

"Oi! Mac! Mac, you knob-head! Over here!" Ollie and Ben were waving madly at him from across the bar. They'd already got a round in and, from the looks of them, had been there some time. They were both well on the way to getting completely pissed.

"We ordered you some chips, buddy," laughed Ollie, "and the finest bottle of champagne the establishment could provide.

We know you're a caviar and ketchup kind of guy. We need to celebrate dude, it's not every day you get promoted to Head of Business Development, you brown-nosing git!"

"Yeah, many con-fucking-gratulations asshole! Now you can do even more work from home on a much higher pay band," Ben snorted, his tie akimbo as he swigged from his pint.

"Seriously though, well done, pal. Guess you'll be picking up all the tabs from here on in, eh?"

Mac chuckled, "Fuck both of you. All right, settle down and let's tone the lingo a tad, people are getting offended over here."

He motioned with his head to the left of him where an older couple were sat scowling disapprovingly.

Ollie leaned around to get a better look.

"Bah, fuck 'em!"

He gave them a little wave and then the finger, chortling when their mouths dropped open in shocked surprise.

Turning his attention back to Mac and Ben, he said, "So, how does it feel to be Mr Bigshot then? Now you can get that twat, Sam, to reel his flamin' neck in, always banging on about KPIs, KPIs and even more KPIs."

"Pretty good," Mac replied. "I am going to make your lives miserable from here on in. I've decided," he paused, snatching up a chip, chewing thoughtfully.

"I'm going to assign you both all the shitty, demanding clients that haggle to the very last penny and make all the project managers cry 'cos they ring up daily demanding a status report. The ones that say, *'we need Scrum'*, and then change their minds and say: *'actually Kanban works just fine, but aren't they actually both Agile'*?

Your favourite ones, Ben, who spout out *jargonlish* at every meeting but couldn't find their arse with both hands if they tried, and they *still* get paid fat packets to act and talk like muppets."

He smirked at them. "And you two numpties will both thank me for it because it will teach you all you need to know about control, manipulation, pathological lying ..." Mac picked up another chip and popped it in his mouth.

"Oh, and brown-nosing. All the *important* qualities of a sales pro," he smiled. "Then you'll be able to shove KPIs up Sam's arse too!"

Ben raised his glass aloft. "Wonderful! I'll drink to that!" He enthused. "Cheers, pal."

"Let's get that bubbly open," Ollie burped.

After much raucous banter and two more plates of chips, both Ollie and Ben were beginning to slur. Mac, who had been pacing himself, was content sipping a diet Coke.

He had allowed himself only a flute of champagne, handing the bottle to the other two to finish off. *'A busy morning tomorrow,'* Mac had informed them, but Ben and Ollie hadn't really cared at that point; they were both having far too much fun, hooting and joking, celebrating Mac's success.

"Soooooo, bud, have you done much more work on that decrepit, old house you bought up in the sticks?" Ollie drawled.

"Yeah, it's blimin' creepy-looking, pal. I reckon it's haunted; you should get that Yvette Fielding in there or maybe that Derek Acorah," Ben mused.

"Nah, not Acorah, bud," Ollie chipped in, winking salaciously, "he hasn't got tits and he's definitely not as much fun to wank over!"

"Put a sock in it, Ollie! You're such a sad sack. Women are more than just tits, you know. No wonder you can never get laid!" Ben retorted, frowning in mock condemnation.

"I'll put a sock *on* it…" Ollie began.

Ben rolled his eyes, shaking his head.

Taking another noisy gulp from his glass, he

eyed Mac sat across the table. "But yeah, Mac my man, why on earth would you want to buy that tumbledown shack?" he continued.

"Fucking spiders and shit running around in there ... What possessed you? Ha! That was fucking good! What possessed you!" Ben spluttered at his own joke.

"If you must know, it's an excellent investment opportunity and that *'ramshackle, haunted shack'* as you so eloquently put it, will make me a fucking killing. It's a renovator's wet dream," Mac responded, his eyes glinting as his mouth upturned smugly in a knowing grin. "There's money to be made in them thar hills, boys."

"He keeps all his freaky stuff there, Ben," Ollie quipped. "You know, his gimp mask and whips!"

Both Ollie and Ben burst out laughing.

"That would be a hell of a sight, Mac, you all kitted out in PVC, ball-gag in your fizzog and feathers in your ass!" Ollie howled, his face creased up in mirth as Ben cackled and then coughed and spluttered, almost spitting his beer out.

"Yes! I can see it now. Mac's Rubs and Scrubs has a certain ring to it. You'd make a fortune, me ol' mucker!" Ollie added gleefully.

Mac chuckled along with them good-naturedly, "I suppose I would look rather fetching in a pair of black chaps. Not sure how I feel about those feathers though!"

"Well, if all else fails, Mac, like ... I don't know ... like if Sam the twat nicks your job, or your ramshackle hut ... apologies, *'investment'*... falls to pieces, you can always open up a restaurant," Ben advised. "Ommpph, 'scuse me!" he let out a hearty belch.

Getting to his feet, wobbling with inebriation, he thumped his chest with a fist dramatically before proclaiming, "your vol-au-vents are legendary, and your mini pies are, mmmmwah!" pinching his fingers and thumb together into an 'ok' shape, Ben raised them to his lips and then tossed them away, kissing the air in the manner of a (very drunk) French chef.

"Sit down, you ass! You look like a right wanker!" Ollie grabbed Ben by his shirt sleeve and tugged him back onto his chair. Ben slouched across the table, face down on his crossed arms, and mumbled something incoherent.

"Never underestimate the power of food when ingratiating yourself to the masses," Mac clicked his tongue. "It's a skill. Tantalise their taste-buds and people trust you so much more."

"Yeah, sure they do...," Ollie trailed off. "Those nibbles you brought over to Stu's party a couple of weeks back though … dude … they were *AH-mazing*. Haven't eaten something tasting as good as that, not for a looooooong time. And I ate Laura, man, know what I'm saying?"

Ollie chugged the remainder of his beer and peered at Mac. "What did you put in them, bud? Pulled pork or something?"

Ollie hiccupped, his eyes swimming. Looking down at his hands for a brief second, Mac raised his head and putting on a creepy voice, said,

"I could tell you, but I'd have to kill you."

"Oh, do one, you dick.

You're suave but not 007 suave, mate! Come

on bud, whaddya' use?" Ollie insisted. "Actually, I use that old house to hide corpses. I like to string women up by their feet like pigs, cut their throats and watch their blood pour out onto the floor. Then I slit them from groin to gullet over a big plastic barrel and pull their stinking guts out with my bare hands.

After that, I strip the flesh off the bones using a fileting knife and a cleaver. I freeze the meat and, when I get hungry, I cook it and eat it. I own them completely. When I run out, I find a fresh pig to slaughter. I'm generous so I share ... I do so love seeing people blissfully unaware they are chomping on Sandra's fillet, Judy's rib chop or Emma's buttocks" Mac said, deadpan.

His mouth slightly agape, Ollie was stunned into a shocked silence. Ben blearily looked up from the table, his face quizzical. He nudged Olliesharply in the ribs. The two men looked at each other for a moment, puzzled. And then burst into fits of riotous laughter. Mac laughed heartily with them, leaning over the table to slap Ben playfully on the back, and show Ollie a double thumbs up.

"Jesus Christ, Mac! That's fucking dark even for you, you weirdo!" Ollie exclaimed, banging his fists on the table. "Fuck dude, have you ever thought of writing horror movies? I'm never eating any of your nibbles ever again, mate, not after tonight! Lecter's got nothing on you!"

"Your faces! Such a picture, the pair of you!" Mac sniggered, "I should have filmed it." He drew a finger across his throat, making a gagging sound as he did so. "One last round before we call it a night, what do you say?" he asked.

"Yeah, you oddball, one more for the road," Ollie answered, still tittering. "Better make Ben's a J2O though, mate, he's dead in the water. Look at 'im!"

"Good idea," Mac responded. "I think I'll have a stiff one ..."

Ollie choked back a snort: "Pwwwt! Mac, you're a fucking card, mate. Gimme your wallet, I know you're loaded, you jammy bugger."

***

He shoved her violently inside and the door slammed shut. Loudly. Abruptly. Metal scraped on metal-like fingernails on a blackboard as the heavy-duty bolt slid and then clanked into place, sealing her in from the outside world. Away from her boyfriend; away from the living; away from salvation.

The room, dimly lit by a miserable little bulb hoisted high up on the ceiling, was filthy.

The industrial tiles felt cold and sticky, smeared with God only knows what.

The walls - just bare, crude brick – were rough and crumbling in places. And the smell, Christ, that smell. It reeked.

She lay there on the floor in a heap, her beautiful, purple sweater with the diamante neckline covered in vomit, her grey leggings torn on both knees. Her blonde hair had unfastened, clumps of it pulled out during the struggle, and her mouth was smeared with her bright, red lipstick, paradoxically clown-like.

Terrified, her breathing came in short, ragged gasps as she took in her immediate surroundings.

Trapped animal-eyes darted about wildly as she struggled to see in the poor light. Too frightened to move even an inch, she could hear the thud of heavy footsteps receding. She would soon be alone…

THE END

The Brown Paper Envelope
Quentin Cope

Part One

How he had waited this long without literally killing someone was beyond him. He tapped his fingers on the crowded desk-top in an irregular, confused rhythm; a strangely disjointed tempo tracking the dark thought processes of someone about to make a life changing decision.

This was a time for focus; selecting the right words and ensuring the right emphasis. He sat hunched over his laptop, a device balanced carefully on a timber shelf only just wide enough to take its full depth. Manipulating words had never been his strong point, but today he would need to make a special effort. Today it would be essential that he get his message across as he had never needed to do before.

Edward Pickering sat locked and secure in his totally unsatisfactory home 'office' during his deliberations; a windowless room and a cramped space of self-banishment. This might well be considered a place of enforced isolation by others and yet it was a situation of his own making, choosing to spend much of his 'at home' time barricaded within the space beneath the stairs.

Although the family had moved house only a few years previously, he had ended up in a poorly designed and imperfectly built property he was not happy with, wondering how the hell he let them badger him into allowing the whole damn family to move in there. The expression 'an insignificant semi in suburbia' summed up the accommodation situation exactly. He wanted it not to be so of course; oh, how he wanted that ... but from his own point of view the situation had been forced upon him and there appeared to be no way back.

Edward however faced a particularly different dilemma, hence the blackness of his mood and his desire to isolate himself from others when at home. On his regular visits to the local pub, he had listened to tales of woe similar to his own and taken the time to study, in some depth, what reactions might have been considered fair and balanced, and what reactions may have been seen as totally inappropriate.

As for the rest of it, well 'family' played its part of course, and in Edward's particular case this consisted of two constantly screaming, out-of-control kids; a dog that barked when it shouldn't and didn't bark when it should, and finally the mother to this brood of unruly individuals, his wife of twenty years ... Christine.

One enlightening fact he had distilled from his many hours of deliberation in the pub was that there always had to be someone to blame. This was a useful revelation as he needed someone to shoulder responsibility for what was about to happen today. It certainly could not be 'him', could it? He was the injured party; the one abused as a result of a conspiracy amongst others.

'Yes' ... he told himself, time and time again. They were to blame for his current predicament, and he had become reconciled to the fact. It was because of 'them' he needed to shoe-horn himself into his 'below stairs' private space every time he wanted a bit of peace and quiet. It was not only an act of determined isolation; it was also one of insulation. Because of 'them' he had been press-ganged into the purchase of a totally unsatisfactory home, the reason being its closeness to a particularly high performing school and the convenience of a quick run by car to the council offices where Christine worked. His opinion about the welfare of his family and most decisively, where they should all live, had been taken away from him as they all gradually ground him down until he offered little or no resistance.

He didn't know what his wife really did at work in any sort of detail and felt unable to compute why she needed to be religiously on-time at her office every damn day. Was she the boss, or wasn't she? Surely in her elevated position she had no need to explain to anyone why she might not appear spot on the stroke of nine o'clock. She had tried to explain it all; her valued position within the hierarchy of the council and her determination to 'lead' her team by example. However, as she was forced to tell him, on a regular basis, unless he showed a modicum of bloody interest, then he would never understand why they paid her so much damned money.

Looking back to when they first met, part of the instant attraction appeared to be the fact they were both so dissimilar. But then each other's circumstances were significantly different; he earning a considerable regular income as a contractor and she a penniless university student.

One thing was for sure; by now far too much water had flowed beneath the creaking bridge and he had finally convinced himself he must make the effort to put everything in the past behind him.

'Things are about to change around here!' Edward repeated to himself several times within the confines of the airless space; his drumming now a fraction louder as the tips of his fingers became numb and desensitised to the abuse. The past had been an experience that had been lived and now he must file it mentally under 'no going back' or 'must not recall'.

With his focus finally redirected, Edward began tapping away much more productively at the keyboard of his laptop; the screen glow illuminating a determined face, an intense look, a display of unrestrained concentration. He simply must get the damn words right!

The email he was busy preparing must be perfect in content and tone. After all, he had exchanged the increasing isolation he felt within his marriage for the physical isolation of understairs habitation and there could be no denying the fact this had become a most difficult pill to keep on swallowing.

There would be no second chances!

The more he thought about it, the more he knew the two of them would be shocked. Yes, they would definitely both be shocked ... but not perhaps in equal measure. There could be no rebuttal, no answer to their situation; a possibly comfortable arrangement once revealed by him and then for the whole damn world to see. Neither of them would have any worthwhile response to the accusation; theories about which he had been assembling for some time inside his unheated, windowless, understairs and isolating space everyone laughingly called his 'office'.

The suspicions had begun to haunt him close to a year ago. A trite phrase here, a scathing look there and times when he desperately wanted to listen to what she might be telling him … but found himself left with nothing constructive to consider. Her attempts at any form of physical contact fell on stony ground which became even stonier as the evidence mounted in Edward's mind. This general decline in their relationship, along with some other burgeoning communications issues, helped to raise his suspicions and feed his increasing anxiety. Did they believe for one single minute, with their high-powered jobs and their fancy university degrees, they could get away with it? He may only be a lowly self-employed joiner, but he too had a brain and what's more, he knew how to use it.

Finally, it was finished. All the right words and all in the right order, spell checked and formatted so that no-one could find fault with it.

Although the final version may have been considered a little short, he thought its content to be to the point and free of any over-inflammatory language.

Time to do it!

He read the email for the tenth time that morning, finger hovering above the 'send' key. The kids banged a couple of times on the locked door to their father's 'office' as they made their way out of the house and into the waiting school transport.

They both shouted:

"Bye, dad!"

There would be no expectation of a reply or any verbal encouragement from a father who really wanted to wish them a successful day but could never find the right level of language. He had considered many times whether they knew ... or not. Had they begun to treat him differently ... but differently to what? They had always considered him to be in some state of despair, a condition perhaps best treated with a certain amount of pity. Their mother had always been the centre of their world and as Edward's sense of isolation became increasingly pronounced, they began to turn even more to their mother for their every need.

Once the children were out the door, Christine would be running up the stairs, coffee in one hand, toast in the other; eager to 'put her face on' and transform herself into someone else. Did that 'someone else' have a name? Edward doubted she would want to countenance the day as plain old Mrs. Christine Pickering. No. She would prefer going back to being the beautifully presented and ambitious Christine McGregor; the name she was born with and the person she was when she first met Edward Pickering. Back to the days when they first met; halcyon days of too much of everything; back to the revealing close-fitting dresses, tantalising aromas, five-inch heels and a nearly insatiable sexual appetite.

However, some twenty plus years on, the low-cut, close-fitting dresses were no more, having disappeared from sight along with uncomfortable high heels and any sign of untamed sexual passion.

Edward read the body of the email once again, convincing himself this would be the very last time. The crucial communication, the one that would kick-start it all, stared threateningly back at him through the reflective screen glow of his laptop. This would be the seventh or eighth time in the past ten minutes. 'Why was he hesitating?' he asked himself. It was time to crap ... or get off the bloody pot. He began yet another read-through ... his hand remained hovering. Finally, with all the courage he could summon, he pressed the 'send' key, pulling back immediately after as if suddenly considering the decision to be misjudged. He began to sweat.

'There, the damn job was done!'

Part Two

Christine would have to make the best of a bad thing. Her choices, however, were particularly limited and for some strange reason less palatable today than normal. Her hair had become more difficult to style and control, and her skin had finally lost any trace of its normal healthy glow. The inexplicable waves of supreme tiredness had also started to become regular events, often lasting multiple wearying minutes at a time. This was probably the most worrying part as such episodes were also becoming more difficult to disguise and trickier to snap out of. Determination had come to her aid many times recently, but even that appeared to have been moderated by an increasing loss of focus. The day would come when one of these 'events' would occur whilst driving her car ... but so far luck had been on her side.

She took one long last look at herself in the mirror. This particular reflection, the one looking back at her, would have to last the whole damn day. The dress, styled to be loose-fitting, disguised increasingly poor muscle tone; the shoes low-heeled and unflattering, proving an attempt to guard protesting feet from the painful effects of increasingly poor circulation.

She heard movement downstairs. That would be Edward extracting himself from his 'office' and making his third cup of tea of the day.

This far from perfect mirrored manifestation of an extraordinarily well-paid local government executive would have to do. She had a busy day ahead, and it already started to go downhill with the onset of a major headache.

"Would you like a cup of tea, dear?" he asked, as she appeared in the kitchen with a look on her face signalling her mind to be obviously elsewhere. His eyes followed her round the room. What was he looking for? What secrets did he expect such surveillance to reveal?

"No, thank you, I'm having coffee this morning. I need the damn caffeine."

She attempted a smile. The lips moved in some sort of reconfiguration but the outcome would remain thin and unconvincing.

He paused in his efforts to decipher any hidden message in her declaration to need the 'damn caffeine'.

"There's some mail for you."

He looked up from the newspaper spread out in front of him, wanting to catch any possible reaction from her; a twitch, a sharp sideways movement of the head or even pursed lips giving the game away as to the contents.

"It's another of those plain brown paper envelopes again, dear. You've had one or two of those lately …"

"Yes, you are absolutely correct, and you will note, dear husband, they have all been addressed to me. So, they are none of your bloody business!"

The words were delivered firmly but without any particular malice. However, to him they appeared scathing and inappropriate and a signal she may be prepared to do battle.

Her eyes rested on the envelope only briefly. She didn't pick it up. It just lay there in the middle of the kitchen table ... taunting him. Was this meant as a warning to Edward; the subject of brown paper envelopes being 'out of bounds'... and not a matter for further discussion?

He returned his attention to the newspaper, picking it up and deliberately shielding his face with it, purposely ignoring the envelope, resting on the kitchen table, only inches away from him.

Her phone bleeped for the third time that morning. It appeared to be a message notification. She read it and sighed in response, muttering something unintelligible beneath her breath.

The headache had become pressing, and her left hand turned unbearably cold without any warning. Burying her concern as best she was able, there could be little doubt that Edward had picked up on something.

His expression changed as he lowered his newspaper.

"Something wrong, dear?" he enquired, feigning a modicum of interest.

"It's from the office IT. The mail server is down … yet again!"

He winced. A server problem! Perhaps his mail might not have been received. Perhaps his triumph may not yet be fully achieved this day. Perhaps his plan was destined to fall apart before it had really begun.

"I suspect that means you might well be late home again tonight, dear."

"That's a possibility Edward."

Attached to the reply came a look full of questions and one he would avoid by burying his head back in the newspaper. She knew all about the various scenarios playing through his mind. She knew about the constant doubt and insecurity, all brought on by his confused feelings of depression and isolation rather than evidenced in any specific action on her behalf.

Was she, or wasn't she? Did she, or didn't she? However he might link a series of brown envelopes to the manufactured theories of possible deceit and poor faith in his wife had always been quite beyond understanding for Christine. Maybe they were seen by him as more of a symbol than hard and irrefutable evidence of wrongdoing.

Whatever he might think, her first duty was to her children and until she was sure - really sure - then she would continue to play the game she had become committed to. He would either turn out to be strong enough to handle it ... or he wouldn't.

One thing was for certain, isolating himself from the rest of his family, and retreating to a cupboard under the damn stairs would not solve any of his perceived problems.

Perhaps the contents of the brown paper envelope, now lurking temptingly in front of her, would supply the spark needed to ignite the engine of purpose. It might even push her into making that one final emotion packed decision; a decision that would have some level of effect on every single member of her family, along with just about everyone else she knew.

Care would be required when opening the envelope. Any sign of a tear or flushed cheek would give the game away completely ... and that would not be good.

She had managed to hold off a full-blown interrogation so far, but the contents of today's brown envelope might well be the news she was somehow expecting.

She knew who it would be from. The plain, unmarked, typewritten and recycled paper missive gave it away.

Christine Pickering studied the enclosed letter. Edward raised his head, focusing his stare, searching for anything he might consider to be a clue.

It took less than a minute.

Her eyes left the paper and locked with his.

The gaze provided no message, no content, no poorly disguised emotion coming through, just a cold, blank stare.

"Anything interesting, my dear; anything you want to tell me about in the mysterious brown paper envelope?" he asked; the question delivered in a barely disguised tone of sarcasm.

She turned her head and muttered something unintelligible in reply and taking the letter and the envelope made her way upstairs. Arriving back in the kitchen once more with handbag and coat in hand, she posed the usual query.

"Do you know if you will be late tonight, dear … because if you are, I will arrange to pick up the kids from my mother?"

"No, I can do it. You just concentrate on your pressing executive duties, confident at least one of us will make sure the kids are looked after …"

She slammed her now empty coffee cup on the island worktop. He had gone too far.

"Don't you dare roll that particular dice with me, you bloody hypocrite. It's me who looks after this damn household.

It's me who cleans the home and puts food on the table for all of us … you included!

It's me who nurtures those children, hugs them when they're scared, praises them when they're good and has to discipline them when they're not!

You are unable to do that, my dear, because such activities cannot be effectively carried out whilst sitting in the bloody pub with all your mates, blowing smoke up one another's backsides … or locked in an understairs cupboard as if suffering from a severe case of onset schizophrenia!"

Now Christine was angry … very angry in fact.

Now Christine's headache had become unbearable … completely and mind numbingly unbearable.

Now she had to face the fact the brown paper envelope had delivered some news she did not want to hear.

Now she felt sure if she did not leave that bloody house this very minute, it was possible she might commit murder!

She slammed the door hard behind her leaving her husband speechless. Had he really gone too far this time? Perhaps he had, but something was afoot here. The brown envelopes had arrived at the house before on several occasions during the past nine months. He had never enquired directly as to their contents and would certainly never consider reading any of them. It was the first rule of trust between two people agreeing to live together. He had assumed they were some level of communication between his wife and one other who must remain confidential.

Today, such an all-important rule would be put aside. Now it was his turn to be angry. Whatever might be going on, today must be the day to get to the bottom of it all … and the place to start would be the brown paper envelopes.

Part Three

Edward searched the bedroom. They would be here somewhere. In fact, it took a little time to locate the small collection of four brown envelopes concealed beneath her bedside cabinet.

He opened the top one, the one apparently received two weeks previously. He sat on the bed reading it. Then he read it again. He would read it for the third time before the first tear fell, landing on the trembling page, gradually absorbing the colour of the close typed script. The dull grey recycled paper had been printed and embossed with a crest, beneath which, inscribed in capitals, was a titled name and London Harley Street address. Sir John was writing to confirm their recent meeting at which Christine's medical 'buddy' was present. The news was not good. In fact, he considered the results of her very last scan to be disappointing.

Edward's wife, partner and friend of more than twenty years would probably not live much longer than three months. The aggressive cancerous tumour seated in the middle of her brain would see to that. Drugs were available that might well reduce the effects of its growth and maybe even extend her period of grace by a couple of months, but an extra month or two was all she could hope for.

The other five letters described something of a journey for her. How the hell had he not noticed something might be wrong? How on earth had she managed to get out bed every damn morning and trudge off to her two thousand pound a week job without one word of complaint? More importantly, why had she not bloody well told him!

He took the six thin brown envelopes, each containing one single sheet of paper, and stuffed them in his back pocket. He simply had to right all the wrongs here; he had to talk to his wife and tell her how damn sorry he was, how much he really did love her and to completely ignore the stupid, spiteful email he just sent to the council's chief executive.

He rushed downstairs, back to the kitchen, searching for his phone, the tears flowing freely now as he punched in her number, his mutterings of self-reprimand becoming louder and louder.

'Please leave a message after ....'

He slammed the phone down searching for the redial.

'Please leave a message ...'

"Damn," he shouted at the top of his voice.

He had to leave the house ... now! He had a twenty-mile journey in front of him in that bloody van, an unreliable ten year old vehicle he hated, but for reasons he could never come to terms with, felt loathe to get rid of.

He would keep trying.

Finally, she answered.

He provided no space for her words. No time given over to greetings. Just hearing her voice became immediately unsettling; a calm, controlled voice; a voice of authority bearing down on him as the words piled up inside his brain, eager to escape and end this unbearable nightmare. He blurted and stammered his apologies, begging her forgiveness, cutting off her attempts to interrupt until finally the tears and the guilt completely overcame him ... the supply of words exhausted ... the ensuing silence acting as a full stop in the one-way conversation.

Christine might best describe her reaction as being close to bewilderment. She knew very well Edward harboured considerable negative thoughts relating to her job and even some of the people she worked with.   Never for one moment had she thought her husband would find it necessary to investigate her movements and make assumptions that were to be so damn far from the reality of it all. The brown envelopes and her failure to reveal to him the detail of their contents had never been designed to push his mindset in any particular direction. She also considered the thought she might be sleeping with her boss and engaging with him in weekends 'away' to be quite abhorrent.

"Listen to me Edward," she demanded at the other end of the telephone, "Peter is my medical 'buddy'. He accompanies me on visits to my oncologist and my surgeon. It's something we insist upon at the council. If someone is long-term sick, they are able to ask anyone from work to be their declared medical 'buddy'. This person is freed up from their duties to accompany the sick individual to medical appointments, treatments and any other engagements found necessary. This is requested by our insurance company for all treatments claimed on their council-provided private medical insurance."

Edward could simply not get his head around it all. There were so many damn questions.

"So, can you tell me when it's going to happen?"

He knew, as soon as he allowed the words to pass his lips, it was a clumsy delivery and insensitive enquiry. 'Damn' he shouted at himself within a mind still finding it difficult to absorb everything she had been telling him.

"The medication is not going as well as everyone hoped, including me of course."

He sensed her smile buried somewhere in the delivery.

"We are all working on three months, and this

will be my last day at work. I was going to tell you this evening. I have been putting it off and I apologise for that, but I have also been living in hope that it might be longer. However, today's confirmation from my specialist confirms the situation to be as it is ... and so my dearest Edward, it looks as if we will all have to live with it ... excuse the pun!"

It was too much; far too much to absorb all in one go. His mind had become a whirl, and it was now speeding down a major northern trunk road at over seventy miles an hour!

Part Four

He would have known nothing about it before it happened. All his senses were trapped and bound together within a brain on fire; unable to translate the urgent messages telling him to slow down and, if possible, bring the death trap he was navigating to a controlled and gentle stop. The only physical clue might have been the increasingly poor steering control and irregular drifting of the van back and forth across two lanes of traffic.

The A19 enjoyed a reputation as being a busy road, especially at this time of day. It was also an unforgiving road with many well-known 'black spots' and the 'RTC' as reported by the first policeman on scene, involved the van, an HGV pulling a thirty-tonne load and two cars luckily carrying no passengers.

Edward Pickering, having begun an unsure journey back to life in the back of an air-ambulance, would be diagnosed with a compound leg fracture, a ruptured aorta, a bleed on the brain and other cranial damage requiring him to be kept under permanent sedation.

After extensive surgery and a long time spent in intensive care, his team of surgeons finally agreed it was time for him to be revived. The general medical staff, without exception, commented on the fact their patient had made a remarkable recovery despite a near uncontrollable infection in his leg wounds.

When he became fully conscious, apprised of his situation and how he got to where he now was, he showed high levels of anxiety, requiring further light sedation to calm him. He muttered through it all 'how long ... how long?'

Finally, when awake once more, he was able to ask the question with a mind uncluttered by the debilitating effects of strong opiates and mental anguish.

"How long have I been like this?"

Several gowned and masked people filled the space at his bedside.

One asked: "You mean in total?"

"Yes ... in total!"

"Three months, three weeks and four days!"

"Oh my God" screamed Edward. "What about my wife? What about Christine? Is she still alive? Please, please tell me she is still alive ... she has not left me ..."

"There was no one else in the van with you Edward. Your wife was not there!" someone in the medical team offered in an attempt to settle his immediate confusion but avoid answering the question in its entirety.

"No ... No!" he shouted. "You must have it wrong. She is always with me. Christine is always there ... in the van you say ... in the van? No ... Christine would never be with me in the van. She hated the damn van ... so where is Christine?"

Now there appeared to be some real confusion; now came the sweat of uncertainty, the rapid rise in blood pressure and a heart that beat in tune with the anxiety of it all.

The following silence lasted only a matter of seconds, but to Edward Pickering it seemed like a lifetime. To those collected by his bedside, every single person there had given of their very best to save the life of this unfortunate accident victim. They all knew of his family circumstances, especially the sad situation with his wife, and at one time or another had all prayed to God he would survive.

As they looked on, Edward's thoughts had become random; flashing images of a past life invading every notion; every moment he regarded as 'good' and every treasured moment he had spent with Christine and the children. He opened his eyes several times for short periods thus giving hope to the medics attending him. Every time he did so, the surrounding collection of electronic gadgetry put on a sound and light show consisting of coloured LED patterns and unharmonious bleeping sounds.

The light in the room gradually became brighter; a dazzling, burning brilliance obscuring everything within his vision and so intense he felt himself blinded by it. He cried out, but it was not with pain. For some inexplicable reason the pain had left him, left him to invade another perhaps? He smiled at the thought of it. A hand came from somewhere, reaching out for his. It materialised in front of him as he stretched toward it, his eyes filled with tears, the emotion of expectation now taking complete control. Finally, two hands made contact; he flinched. The touch would be familiar; the voice, the soft and well-articulated tones even more so.

She squeezed gently. He tried to move his head to the left but nothing seemed to be working. Then the tears came in buckets; whether tears of joy or frustration, those living ones surrounding him would never be able to tell.

She spoke.

"My darling man … I have some great news for you!"

THE END

The Cave
Terry (T.R.) Moran

It was two o'clock and since the heat from the midday Sun had eventually cooled, it was finally time to follow his guides into the cave system. Michael had booked this trip over a year ago and had needed to get himself certified to go into such a very dangerous place.

His guides, Simon and Paul, were veteran Cave explorers with a combined forty years experience between them. Michael put on all the necessary safety equipment and then hooked himself up to the lifeline; one that tethered him to the two experts.

Now they were ready to go. With some trepidation, Michael followed Simon into the mouth of the cave as Paul brought up the rear.

The sight that greeted the three men could only be described as breathtaking. An enormous, glistening cavern with stalagmites the size of multi-story buildings appeared as though they were holding up the ceiling of this vast expanse.

"Now ..." Paul said from behind, "we are going to follow the main passages. Some of them are narrow but don't worry, you are very safe with us. If, for any reason, the guideline does come loose, then just stay put and let us deal with it. Don't go wandering off somewhere else."

This elicited a nod of approval from Simon, who glanced over his shoulder at Michael before adding: "Lots of branching paths in there, and yelling won't help us find you. Sounds are funny in here. Something closeby might sound far away … and anything you hear in the distance ..!"

Feeling a sudden thump on his shoulder, Michael whipped around, eyes already wide with fright.

"... might be right behind you!" finished Paul; winking with a larger-than-life smile as he pulled back his huge hand.

Michael rolled his eyes. Since the other two were alternately chuckling or wiggling their fingers while making mocking ghost-like wails.

Catching his breath, Michael nodded in agreement and the three adventurers set off deeper into the cave. At first, the passage had been narrow, barely allowing for the men to walk in single file, though thankfully, after at least a half hour slow and careful progress, the tunnel had widened enough for them to walk together more comfortably as a group.

As they moved forward, Michael found himself gazing in wonder at all the marvelous rock formations and sparkling glints of innumerable small crystals.

"This place is like another world," he said, in awe of the majestic cave.

His two guides exchanged knowing smiles, and in unison they replied: "You haven't seen anything yet."

Paul walked over to Michael, put a hand on his shoulder and whispered,

"This place holds secrets and wonders you'll

not believe real, even when you see them with your own eyes."

At this, Michael's heart began to race with excitement. He had heard of the amazing things people had claimed to have seen in this cave system, but no evidence had ever been provided in the form of photography or film due to the presence of some sort of strange magnetic interference.

Michael didn't really understand all the science babble his friend back home had explained to him, but apparently cameras of any kind, even the brand new digital ones, did not work. Neither did mobile phones, but that didn't matter to Michael. He was here to see these wonders for himself.

The three men carried on walking deeper into the cave, noisily chatting as they went. Suddenly, Simon stopped. He looked straight up, and then toward Paul who quickly grabbed Michael, keeping him secure. They raced over to the shelter of a large stalactite where the three of them hid. Michael looked panicky, eyes darting nervously around the dark cavernous heights above.

"What is it? What did you see?" Paul hissed, looking up to follow Simon's gaze. Michael searched for a long time unable to find whatever his guide had seen, but then Paul shone his torch up to the top of the vast cavern. Michael gasped. "Are are those ...?"

"Yup. Giant bats," Paul interrupted, sighing in relief.

Up in the shadows of the cave ceiling were hundreds of enormous leathery creatures with black wings, all wrapped snugly around their huge sleeping bodies. However, the light that Paul had shone upward to confirm what Simon had seen, looked to have disturbed the creatures. They began to unfurl their massive wings and take flight.

There were so many bats that even though the trio hadn't gone so far into the cavern for the day's sun to fade, the screeching colony now blocked any trace of natural light completely. The bats flew swiftly past, close to their heads. Michael ducked, covering his face with his hands to protect himself as best he could.

However, instead of finding himself terrified, on the contrary; Michael appeared to carry the biggest of smiles on his face. He had never seen such high numbers of large bats in his entire life. When they had finally all flown away, the three men stood up.

"Those things were huge! They must have had at least a six-foot wingspan!" Michael gasped excitedly.

"Five-foot at most' Paul chimed in. "Those are giant fruit bats, also known as 'flying foxes'. Indigenous to this part of the world, and this cave happens to be a very popular roost for them."

"This place is really wondrous. I can't wait to see what's next."

"We had best get a move on then. We don't wanna' miss the light show." said Simon.

Michael found himself intrigued by what his guide had just said, but thought it best not to enquire further in case he potentially spoilt the surprise.

So keeping quiet as possible, the trio made

their way deeper into the cave. After only a few moments, the walls of the vast cavern started to close in and all light from the cave entrance had finally disappeared.

Now they would need to rely on their flashlights as the only source of illumination, and the cave took on a much more sinister feel.

The echo of each step now sounded like a stalker following just one step behind. Shadows cast against the surrounding rock walls might well be hiding some strange and fearfully dark creature. Even the air itself felt thicker, almost as though it was trying to stop the group from venturing any further.

Thankfully, Michael's will to explore was stronger than this new unfounded fear. He followed his guides deeper into the cave. Now, the three men needed to duck their heads as the ceiling dipped dramatically. Walls that were once so distant that Michael could barely see them had now become so close, he almost felt that they wanted to crush him.

"Ok, Michael," Paul began, "I want you to take the lead here. At this, Michael's ears pricked up, listening closely to his instructions. Don't worry, it's a straight walk to the next chamber but I want you to experience its magnificence first, since Simon and I already know what's ahead ..."

Michael felt the tension from their connecting rope slacken at Paul's end, and so began to untie his own guideline; the two men carefully trading places, their bodies pressing up against each other within the confining walls of the tunnel. Eventually, Michael took over the lead and the three men pressed on. Michael carefully made his way along the claustrophobic tunnel until he thought he saw something in the distance.

"Could they be stars?" Michael wondered to himself. "No. That would be insane." He cursed at himself, internally? As he came closer to the end of the tunnel, he saw even more glowing lights and noticed that some of them were moving through the air.

Without turning, he asked "Ok what are those things ... fireflies?"

From behind, he heard a chuckle. "More like fire-dragonflies; a newly discovered species with a similar body structure to dragonflies, but possessing bioluminescent wings. Hence the twinkling effect as light is both reflected and radiated directly from them.

"Better yet ..." the other voice chimed in "As far as anyone knows this is the only place they exist"

"That's incredible ... so we -" Michael was interrupted by a thunderous rumble so loud it sounded like it was coming from everywhere all at once. The fire-dragonflies took to the air, darting in all directions in a desperate attempt to find safety. Then, the cavern walls shook, cracks forming quickly and showing signs of collapse. Michael called desperately to his guides. He felt a sharp pain as he was struck on the head by something heavy and, in an instant, he lost consciousness.

Michael's head pounded; the pain like a stabbing lightning bolt in his brain. Even in the darkness of the cave, attempting to open his eyes left him in excruciating agony. Michael called out to his guides once more, but the only response was his own echo.

He felt around the floor for his torch, bumping his already injured head again in the process. His hands felt around the cold stone floor but found no sign of his light.

"Is anyone there?" he called weakly. Only his echo replied, and as it faded he was all alone once more. Michael stood up as much as he could in the tunnel and realized there was no light, no light at all up ahead.

Gathering his bearings, he walked forward maybe ten paces to find himself up against a solid wall of piled broken stone. He then took a few steps to his right and hit the wall he expected to be there.

"I have to get out of here. I need to find my guides!"

That's when he remembered the rope around his waist. Michael grabbed at that life-saving guideline and with slow, careful steps he walked the length of it.

He held onto a glimmer of hope once more ... that is until, smack! He walked right into a solid pile of fallen rocks.

At that point, his guide rope and his living hope ended, both crushed under the pile of rubble before him. Michael now knew for sure he was trapped in this cave; trapped and alone in the pitch blackness.

Disbelief overtook him first, unable to fathom his own abysmal luck.

Then, despair and dismay completely

overwhelmed him. He sank to the floor of what was now, his tomb.

Isolated from the world, Michael had lost everything, just as he was lost to the world.

He remains there to this very day.

THE END

The Nineteenth Day
A.J. Lot

Part One

Craig Leven Training Facility.

The blow hurt more because it was unexpected rather than the force and energy behind it. The voice had always come at him from the front; the threats, the profanities, the stinking breath, the words screaming at some distance and then whispered, close to the ear, as the ugly indicators of coercion became more explicit. No; for sure the strike came from behind ... so there had to be more than one other in the room.

A second wound opened up at the back of his head. He sensed the familiar wetness spreading down his neck, signalling the next lot of questions might be more difficult to answer. It was possible that heavy fists could well be replaced with more solid instruments of torture and pain.

He waited, his whole body tensed for another assault, but after some minutes, he realised the room had fallen to silence. Had they gone? Had they given up? With hands tied behind him and further restraints holding him to the hard wooden chair, he began to manipulate his hands together in an attempt to loosen the hessian rope bindings. They had made a mistake when they brought him into wherever the hell he was. Plastic tie-wraps, wire or poly-rope would have denied him any possibility of releasing the wrist straps; however, the hessian rope was simply a pliable collection of thin strands, and with some concentrated effort could be made to untwist and eventually break, one by one. It would be a drawn out and painful process, but as long as there were no more mind-numbing blows to his head, he could begin the task.

The vaporous smell hung heavy around him. The sickening mixture of faeces, urine, fetid breath and the stale sweat of unwashed bodies filled what he assumed must be a windowless and airless place. The expected blow did not come, and although he hadn't heard a door close or the tell-tale shuffling of feet across a dusted floor, he assumed his interrogators had left the room ... but for how long?

Perhaps now might be the time to attempt a survey of his confinement, the cruel space that held him in isolation from others. Although he knew his ankles had been tied to the chair legs, with some concentrated effort he felt sure he could shuffle a few inches at a time to make a move forward. But what if they came back whilst he was in the middle of his survey? They would be angry ... and they would punish him.

A decision had to be made. The attempt to examine the limits of his detention would need to take second place to tackling the dry hessian rope strands. This, as it turned out, was to be the right decision.

It took some hours. How long, he didn't really

know. He had no way of estimating with any accuracy but as the final thread gave way to his constant picking, pulling and rotating, he felt the rope holding his wrists slacken to the point where he could slip his right hand through the open fibres and reach for the blindfold. His wrists had been rubbed sore and bleeding and as he grasped the blindfold wrapped tight against his eyes he cried out with pain.

He didn't know of course, but at some stage of the 'interrogation' his right shoulder had been dislocated. He finally brought up his left hand to pull away the cloth revealing nothing but darkness ... complete and utter darkness! It would take several more painful minutes to free his legs and test his weight on them. Inch by inch, he raised himself, praying to God they would not let him down. His feet would be the biggest concern.

They had taken a severe beating and as he lifted himself upward, transferring his whole weight to his legs, he became more confident until managing to stand without any support from the chair whatsoever.

One deep breath later, he shuffled forward until he came up against a cold, damp wall. He felt his way along it until discovering what must have been a solid steel door. With his back to the newly discovered door, he moved forward, toe to heel, measuring the number of steps until he came up against an expected obstacle.

By touch, he knew it would be another wall. It measured fifteen full steps from the door, so approximately fifteen feet away. Moving carefully around the confining space, he now visualised a concrete block-built room, fifteen feet wide by twenty feet deep and accessed by one single, welded steel door.

'There must be a damn light in here', he muttered to himself as he returned to the door and stretched up with his left arm to both sides.

Sure enough, on the wall next to the door and at just above head height, he discovered a surface mounted switch. He flicked it down and a dull, bare low wattage light came on. It hung from the ceiling of the room at about ten feet in height. Now he was cooking with gas ... or so he thought! However, Sergeant Dominic Alvarez had some way to go yet before he might truly declare himself to be safe. One thing was for sure, the next person to make his way in through that door would not be walking back out again anytime soon.

Even with only one good arm, he would be ready. He took the wooden chair and smashed it against the wall, wrenching the legs from the seat. Now he had a weapon; now he waited; now he stood a chance.

Part Two

Alyth Military Hospital.

Alvarez sensed something might be happening around him. He could hear the murmur of voices and considered he might be laying on something warm and soft. He knew his eyes were closed and for some strange reason he couldn't open them. He began to pick up snatches of conversation. Whoever they were, they were talking English.

With all the energy he could muster, he formed the words 'Help Me!' in his mind and shouted them out at the top of his voice.

The murmurings stopped. The words had indeed been released to everyone gathered round that particular hospital bed that day ... but delivered only as a strained whisper. A cool hand touched his forehead. He became immediately absorbed by a magnificent fragrance as she approached; then bending over him, gently releasing his eyelids from the restraining hospital tape. Sergeant Dominic Alvarez of Number 42 Commando, Royal Marines was alive and kicking.

The brightness and the whiteness of his surroundings took some time to absorb, the light initially blinding and painful. The immediate and worrying thought had to be a questioning one. Was this just another part of the same old trick? Were they going to punish him more severely now for trying to escape the dank, foul-smelling chamber of torture he had inhabited for days ... or possibly even weeks?

The military hospital at Alyth, some twenty plus miles north of Perth in Scotland, had recently received a new patient. There was no name on the door to the private suite and an armed soldier had been placed outside the room on a two-hour rotation.

The installation did not look like a hospital from the outside; there were no informative signs and no obvious involvement with the National Health Service. The whole area had been fenced, topped with razor wire and carried signs warning any interested parties that this collection of buildings should be regarded as a Ministry of Defence property, and therefore, out of bounds to just about everyone.

She leant over him, her face gradually falling into full focus. It was a beautiful face; the face of an angel. She stroked his brow, a calming, soothing touch, bringing a tear to his eye.

She spoke.

"There now, my brave soldier ... you are in safe hands. Everyone here is dedicated to making you well."

"How long ...?" he whispered.

"How long have you been here? Well by this afternoon it will be three whole days. You have been in a medically induced coma whilst we patched you up a bit ... but now you appear to be on the mend, and that's what we want you to concentrate on now."

Dominic's face lit up.

"What ... err ... what's your name ...?

"My name is Alice ... and I'm going to give you something to make you sleep for the next hour or so and when you wake up there will be people who will want to have a chat with you. Is that going to be ok Dominic?"

"Anything for you, Alice ... my beautiful girl!"

Senior nurse Alice Donahue laughed out loud as she released the clear chemical anaesthetic into an intravenous line, and less than a minute later Dominic Alvarez had returned to a place where, for the past three days, there had been no pain.

Part Three

Craig Leven Base

Colonel Watson-Wyatt, the most senior officer in the Special Forces Intelligence Unit 16, would describe his mood as bad as it possibly could be. It rained constantly, and the cold penetrated every layer of clothing despite his driver having the heating turned full on. The Colonel felt a shiver overtake him as the Craig Leven Field Training Centre came into view. A razor wire barrier, attended by two armed and soaking wet soldiers, would stop any further progress until identification had been proven and an image of the two visitors recorded on body-worn cameras. The low profile, crudely constructed buildings behind the wire were unlit and unwelcoming. The driver pulled up at a door to the second block back from the perimeter. An informative sign read 'HUT 3 – Staff Only'. The Colonel exited the Land Rover, briefcase in hand, and pushed his way through the door to Hut 3 only to find it was as cold and inhospitable inside as it was out.

"Damn ...!" he shouted to the empty foul-smelling room.

"Is there anyone here for fuck's sake?"

A door opened behind him and two burly individuals entered, one much taller than the other and both wearing identical black overalls and baseball caps. Two pairs of eyes focused on the officer in the room; not necessarily a hostile look, but not a welcoming one either. The bleak space appeared bare of furniture except for a well-used and rickety wooden trestle table surrounded by six uncomfortable looking folding chairs. Watson-Wyatt dusted the seat of one with his glove and sat down.

"I don't want to make a meal of this ... but I reckon you both well and truly fucked up this time!"

The Colonel indicated the chairs in front of him and with a wave of his finger instructed the two men to be seated.

"How is he?" the shorter blank eyed man asked; the voice emotionless, the delivery monotone.

"Alive ... but no thanks to you two" offered the officer who did not look up as he searched for documents and a digital voice recorder in his army briefcase. Once he had collected everything together, the 'on the record' interview would begin. It would take a little longer than three hours. At the end of it the Colonel ended up with a collection of handwritten scribble spread over sixteen sheets of paper and a sound recording containing several noticeable gaps and one or two long pauses in conversation.

Watson-Wyatt threw his pen down. He desperately needed a cup of tea ... but it was not over yet. He addressed his words, 'off the record' to the taller of the two men, Sergeant Dickson.

"You had him in complete isolation in that bloody hellhole for nineteen days; nineteen days tied to a fucking chair, sitting in his own shit and graciously allowed two cups of water a day and two bowls of cold bloody soup. What are you ... some sort of madman?"

Sergeant Dickson was unsure as to whether such a question needed an answer.

"I told him, sir ... I bloody well told him ... I did, didn't I, Billie?"

The words were spoken by the shorter man, Corporal Black; someone who had appeared agitated and nervous throughout the whole proceedings. His brow displayed a betraying, glistening dampness and his movements had become jerky and restless. He knew what might well be at the end of this meeting in terms of discipline, and he had a family to consider. Billie Dickson was a career soldier, unmarried and disentangled from emotion. He was a career man and lived, ate and slept the Special Forces.

'They wouldn't throw him out,' considered Corporal Black. 'They needed animals like him to do the sort of jobs they could easily deny ... carried out in places they were not supposed to be.'

"So Billie, off the record, what went wrong with this one? We've been doing interrogation exercises and training here for a long time and you have been the senior instructor for more than a year. The others passing through here might well have found it tough, but nobody has been subjected to that length of isolation and the hospital report makes for some bloody grim reading."

Sergeant Dickson remained straight backed in his chair, unblinking and looking directly ahead, avoiding any eye contact with the Colonel. He remained silent.

"Are you listening to me for fuck's sake? The list of injuries would be less if he had spent time with the bloody Taliban. Broken fingers, dislocated arm, thirty-five stitches in his scalp, a bleed on the brain, a broken ankle, bruised kidneys and two crushed fingernails on his left hand! What the hell were you thinking of man ..."

"I told him sir ... I fucking well told him ... didn't I, Billie? You can't blame any of this on me, sir, I ..."

"Shut-up for God's sake, corporal. As far as I'm concerned, you were in the damn room ... so you are just as responsible ... and now I recommend you be quiet!"

The officer turned his attention back to Dickson.

"I wish to exercise my right to remain silent, sir."

"Well, I can do no more here if you won't talk to me, sergeant. The both of you will now need to return to the Credenhill base. A chopper will collect you from here tomorrow morning. At the moment you are both detained and under investigation. As far as anyone else is concerned, this matter now comes under the Official Secrets Act and is to be discussed with no-one; is that clear?"

The hearing took place two weeks later in Hereford at the Stirling Lines Garrison, Credenhill. This was the home of 22 Special Air Service Regiment, and the disciplinary panel would be led by a Colonel from the Marines sitting with Watson-Wyatt and a major from the Welsh Guards. As expected, it turned out to be a grim-faced affair and lasted two days. After some hours of deliberation, the tribunal panel came to a conclusion that certain lines had been crossed; excess violence had been used on Alvarez and that he had undergone unnecessary physical and mental abuse. Corporal Black had refused to speak or offer any explanation for the methods used to 'interrogate' Sergeant Alvarez, as he was just 'following orders'!

He was found guilty of joint enterprise, stopped two weeks' pay and demoted to Lance Corporal. Sergeant Dickson, however, had a lot to say. He even questioned whether or not the panel had any right to be formed under Army Regulations as a tribunal. This did not go down well, and his legal representative advised, most strongly, that he take another path in defending his actions.

"On this particular exercise we were required to simulate interrogation techniques used by a particular enemy in order to test the mental resolve of applicants. This group were all soldiers in other regiments wanting to move over to the Special Forces ... and as such, we always came down on them a little harder.

All Alvarez had to do, to stop the whole fucking process dead in its tracks, was to give us the codeword. That's all he had to do. The word we wanted was 'Firebrand,' but the stubborn bastard would not give in ... he would not bloody well give in sir ... and that is where the problem rests. You ask Alvarez why he would NOT give me the bloody codeword!"

No-one would ever get to the bottom of that particular issue, especially the panel sitting in judgement on the two soldiers. Sergeant William

(Billie) Dickson was found guilty on seven counts ranging from disobeying orders to malicious wounding and as a result was demoted to Lance Corporal with loss of seniority, six months' detention and docked one month's pay. Would that be the end of it? Surely not!

Part Four

Three years later.

Dominic Alvarez enjoyed his life in Benidorm. With a Spanish father and English mother, he spoke the national languages of both perfectly and this was to be a keystone to the success of his real estate business, Alvarez Properties. He had family living close by in Alicante; his mother and two younger brothers. His father had sadly died of a liver malfunction some years previously ... and Dominic missed him like hell. Having left the British Armed Forces in receipt of a substantial financial settlement, about which his lips were sealed, Dominic, still happily single, was about to open his third office in the more northern coastal town of Denia. Although he had worked hard to put the memory of some particularly painful experiences behind him, there was no doubt Dominic Alvarez had suffered physical and mental torture at the hand of the British military. The experience had left him with one or two indelible scars; psychological scars that even with the benefit of time he had found impossible to erase.

Two doors down from his Benidorm premises, the Cafe Verde had become Dominic's favourite place to relax, have a re-energising cup of coffee and a scan of the National newspapers kept clean and unused for him by the cafe owner, Miguel.

On this particular day both men appeared relaxed and in good humour as they chatted together seated at one of the pavement tables. It was pre-season in Benidorm, but with the arrival of Easter in two weeks' time the whole place would be invaded by holiday makers and then the hard work and long days would begin. As people passed by Cafe Verde, Dominic eyed them one by one; not for any particular reason but just in the normal mood of 'people watching'.

A tall, well-built man in shorts and wearing a brightly-coloured sleeveless shirt wandered by. The hairs on the back of Dominic's neck stood up; alarm bells jingled away in the background. The conversation with Miguel came to an abrupt halt as Dominic's eyes focused on the man now sitting about a hundred yards away at a table outside the 'Tivoli' Restaurant & Bar. An eager waiter quickly descended on him and a minute or two later served the stranger with a large beer.

Did the outline of the man in the distance look familiar? Yes, it did. Dominic took out his phone, focusing the camera on the distant figure, zooming in until the face became clear. There could be no doubt about it. This was the man Dominic thought he knew except since they last met, he had collected a very ugly looking scar down his left cheek. This was William (Billie) Dickson, full time member of the shady and secretive British SAS and part time torturer. Miguel could tell something was up with his friend and remained silent as Dominic silently studied the image on his mobile phone.

"Everything Ok?" the cafe owner queried.

"Everything is fine, my friend. It's just that man outside the Tivoli looked familiar ... but studying him a bit more closely he's not the person I thought he was."

Dominic offered a weak smile and a lacklustre gaze in defence of the lie, and Miguel logged the incident as worth remembering. The two men parted, both with the excuse of 'work' calling them away. Dominic returned to his office and opened the software designed to manage his office security system. He refocused the camera directed down the 'calle peatonal' until he had a clear picture of William (Billie) Dickson. He remained sitting outside the 'Tivoli' Restaurant & Bar reading what appeared to be an English newspaper. Alvarez took an image of the man he knew to be Dickson and printed it out. Yes. There could be no doubt. It was him, and what Dominic Alvarez needed now was a plan.

He watched the image on the screen for a further fifteen minutes before Dickson raised himself, shouted something to the waiter and with a wave, ambled off down the road with newspaper in hand.

He appeared to be in no hurry and with Dominic Alvarez a suitable distance behind, made his way to the Sol Vista Hotel where he collected a key from reception and headed for the lifts.

A quiet discussion with the duty receptionist in Spanish revealed the room number of someone named Daniel Pickering who had checked in the day before. From his booking details, he was scheduled to stay for a couple of weeks.

'Plenty of time', thought Dominic.

Now an element of patience would be required whilst a plan came together. He would follow his 'target' day and night until he could find a pattern in his movements; some regular activity or even a regular inactivity. With all plans to reform the new Denia office now on hold, Dominic devoted all his time to the surveillance of Dickson masquerading as Daniel Pickering and by the end of the week, he had a plan.

It quickly become obvious the Englishman's time in Benidorm was to be consumed by drinking and chasing any opportunity for having sex. After steadily drinking all day, Dickson would spend the evening, and most of the night, attending his favourite night spot ... 'La Follies'.

Part Five

Cueva del Agua.

Six o'clock in the morning had been ruled kicking-out time at 'La Follies' and Romero Montez, the manager, remained strict regarding that one simple rule. At six fifteen, the Guardia would be along to check the premises, and the building would need to be empty. At the rear were eighteen rooms better described as 'cubicles' with each containing a double bed, a toilet and a cupboard filled with 'accessories' and 'disposables'.

Dickson had been long gone by the time Alvarez made himself known to Montez. With a couple of fifty Euro notes in his back pocket Romero was quite happy to confirm the Englishman they all knew as Daniel Pickering would arrive about midnight, buy the girls a drink or two, choose one and then retire to room number eleven, paying for any extras and sometimes two girls at the same time. He came to the club every night he holidayed in Benidorm and the routine had always been the same. Dominic Alvarez thanked the co-operative club manager and added an extra fifty euro note to ensure there would be no lingering memory of the conversation.

The drive to his family property in Alicante later that day turned out to be an unexpectedly pleasant one for Alvarez. The sun shone on a low horizon, the traffic remained refreshingly light and the temperature a healthy twenty-two degrees. As Dominic turned off the motorway, he couldn't resist a glance to his right bringing into focus the distant mountains, home to the busy working town of Almansa. He knew this whole area well, being raised there as a child.

His mother, who still spoke a hesitant form of Spanish, even after all these years, preferred her family conversations to be in English. In the well-maintained garden of the Alicante family home. Mother and son chatted and consumed the obligatory coffee and sticky cakes. They sat close together with Dominic frequently placing a comforting arm around her shoulder and promising to visit again sometime the following week.

Before leaving, he recovered a shoe sized tin box from its well-hidden place in the garage along with a cloth bag containing a set of abseiling gear and a couple of hundred feet of lightweight rope. He placed it all in the trunk of his car. The second part of his plan had now been completed and Dominic Alvarez carried with him a smile of quiet determination. He would make a couple of detours before finally heading for home.

The first would be to a Chinese 'we sell everything' shop on the outskirts of town where he bought and paid cash for three strong hessian shopping bags, a hundred-and-fifty-foot-long reel of plastic-coated twine, nineteen small bottles of still water and nineteen bars of chocolate.

The second detour would be to a place he played as a child known locally as 'Cueva del Agua'. It was a remote location in an area difficult to navigate, but Dominic knew how to get to it and after doing what he needed, made his way back down to the autoroute ... and then home.

Next day and back in Benidorm, Dickson had consumed his first beer of the morning at his favourite fuel stop, the 'Tivoli' Restaurant & Bar ... and as Dominic watched on, he began to demolish his second. If everything went to plan, the Englishman would not be here, sipping on his ice-cold beer tomorrow ... but he would sure as hell wish he was!

At his Benidorm apartment, Dominic emptied the tin box recovered from the family garage and spread it across the kitchen table. It contained a Glock 17 Luger handgun wrapped in an oiled cloth along with three clips of 9mm ammunition; a stun gun with a fifty-thousand-volt charge and strong enough to bring down a small elephant; a packet of plastic cable-tie restraints and a Swiss Army knife. Tonight, or more correctly the early hours of tomorrow morning, would be the last time William (Billie) Dickson would be visiting the brothel stroke nightclub on the Avenue de la Valenciana, known as 'La Follies'.

When he exited the building at his normal time of around four o'clock, he would turn left down Avenida del Placio where he regularly parked his hire car. However, on this particular morning, to get to his vehicle, he would need to pass a dark blue and somewhat battered looking Ford Transit van. It belonged to Pedro Gonzales, a painting contractor who regularly carried out work for Alvarez Properties. Dominic had arranged to borrow it for the night ... and now all he had to do was to wait!

Half an hour earlier than expected, Dickson appeared in the distance. He looked a little unsteady on his feet and stopped two or three times, head bowed and studying the pavement for a second or two, as if fighting the effects of light-headedness. Dominic had prepared himself for a difficult capture. Even working simply on instinct, the Special Forces soldier coming his way would be more than capable of putting up a good fight. He perhaps had only one real chance of overcoming the target and bundling him into the side door of the van. He couldn't afford a fuck up!

As Dickson moved up in line with the van, the side door silently drew back on well-oiled sliders and Alvarez jumped out, the stun gun gripped firmly at the end of an outstretched arm. Immediately, Dickson became alert, his eyes capturing the gaze of his adversary. The confirmation of his recognition came with just one word: "Alvarez ..."

Dominic pulled the trigger, and his target slumped to the floor. Although Alvarez kept himself fit and active, manhandling the deadweight of Billie Dickson proved difficult. It took some time to heave the unresponsive body into the van, fit the cable-tie restraints to ankles and wrists and 'hog tie' the two together. The final act would be to lever open the mouth of an already drunk victim and force half a bottle of brandy down his throat.

An hour later, the rusting and dented dark blue Ford van turned off the main coastal road behind Alicante and headed inland toward Almansa. Turning off the main road once more, Dominic headed down a track that would take him behind the village of Torre. He needed to get to his final destination before sunrise. The last kilometre would be a difficult drive and Dominic wondered if the ill-maintained and ancient van would be able to make it.

Eventually the final destination came into view. To the untrained eye there would not be much to see, but Dominic knew that hidden in amongst the various rock outcrops and pinnacles was the entrance to a cave; a cave better described as a pothole perhaps and known to Dominic as the 'Cueva del Agua'.

The space that defined its entrance he knew to be about thirty feet wide. Its depth had been measured at seventy feet and a constant flow of ice-cold water ran through the bottom and across a narrow shelf in winter.

However, today the bottom of the cave would be dry. Manhandling Dickson out of the van and up to the rim of the cave entrance took too much time and a great deal of effort.

The sun had begun to rise, and Dominic needed to be well away from there. With the bottled water and chocolate lowered down into the blackness of the cave using the shopping bags and twine, it was time to prepare William (Billie) Dickson for what lay ahead. He rested with his head only inches away from the edge of the dark void. He wasn't unconscious, but he definitely was suffering the effects of the brandy combined with a night of heavy drinking. Dominic bent down and whispered in the soldier's ear.

"This won't take much longer, Billie."

He reached out with the army knife and cut the plastic tie linking the wrists and ankles.

"I'm pushing you over the edge of this damned hole, Billie and it's a fucking long way down. However, if you survive the fall, I have left some rations for you; nineteen days of rations Billie; nineteen bottles of water and nineteen bars of chocolate ... if you can find a way out of the restraints, of course.

You will no doubt remember the number nineteen as this was the number of days you held me, beat me, tortured me and fed me cold soup. I will be back in nineteen days' time to see if you have survived. If you have, I will lift you out of your confinement. If not, I will leave your useless body to rot right here in your own fucking mess. I hope you can hear this, Billie. It's time to say goodbye!"

With one sustained effort, Dominic finally managed to roll the un-cooperative, drunken body, feet first over the edge, into the blackness and damp oblivion of his captivity.

Part Six

Nineteen Days.

For the next two weeks, Dominic had little time to think about anything other than opening his new office in Denia. Dealing with the local 'mafia' ended up being tougher than expected. To make a breakthrough he voted for a partnership with one of the three biggest land owning and property families in the area, and once agreed, everything suddenly became 'plain sailing'.

With staff for the Denia office under training in Benidorm and internal decorations receiving their final touch, Dominic set the date of the official opening of Alvarez Denia for seven days' time. With invitations sent, radio stations booked for promotional interviews and sales teams chasing the market for new clients, Dominic Alvarez had achieved all his targets ... except for one. The issue of William (Billie) Dickson played on his mind and now he had more time, it became an increasing distraction. If the scenario was to play out to its full and proper conclusion, there were just two days to go out of the nineteen promised to the English soldier.

Dominic Alvarez had his climbing and abseiling equipment in the boot of his car. He had promised his mother he would visit her in Alicante that morning and, therefore, it would be no great issue to make a detour to the cave. Yes, his mind had been made up. Curiosity had won the day. He would visit Dickson. The journey would take just over an hour. As he turned the matter back and forth in his mind, he felt no particular emotion; no sympathy, no anger and little or no satisfaction. He had a job to do ... and he had done it. Now he must face the outcome and deal with it.

A couple of cups of strong coffee and one or two sticky cakes forced Dominic to declare to his mother that it was time to go. He had things to do in Alicante town and much as he loved her company, he needed to leave her. Dominic kissed his mother on the cheek and as he drew away, he had a strange feeling ... a frightening feeling; a feeling as if this might be the last time he would see her. He looked into her eyes; they were bright and shining; incapable of telling lies.

"Are you feeling well, Mother? Is there something you are maybe not telling me?"

She focused in on him as he drew away.

"Of course not, Son, I am as fit as a fiddle ... as you can clearly see!"

She gave out one of her wonderfully reassuring smiles and although not totally convinced, Dominic pushed his concerns to the back of his mind. He needed to be on his way to the cave. He was becoming impatient with the situation he found himself in!

Dominic Alvarez was not a slow or hesitant driver, but he considered himself a cautious one, especially when navigating the notorious road junction at the Poligono Babel. The junction would link him to the A-31 Autoroute out of Alicante and in the direction of Almansa.

The journey took longer than planned and Dominic would be forced to abandon his car and climb the last few hundred feet to the cave. He had his Glock 9mm stuffed in his waistband, his knife in his pocket and his climbing rope over his shoulder. He checked the outside rim of the cave entrance to see if there had been any disturbance. He couldn't really tell but there were no obvious signs. Then a voice, an unexpected voice, came at him from behind. Did he recognise it? He should have.

"Don't turn round."

The instruction was clear.

"Have you come to rescue me ... or bury me, Mr. Alvarez?"

"I have come to bury you, Dickson ... but now it looks as if I will have to shoot you first.

Whatever you may be as a man Dickson, you sure as fuck are an unbelievable survivor!"

Dominic turned quickly, reaching behind him for his Glock pistol.

The sight that greeted Alvarez initially shocked him; the gaunt face, the hideously lean frame, the hands bloody and malformed, the posture stooped and favouring his left side. He stood on a small ridge about fifteen feet away holding a rock that appeared to be consuming most if not all the strength he had left in his near unrecognizable and battle-scarred body. He raised the rock up to chest height; sweat pouring in rivulets, reflecting the level of determination. He screamed out loud with the effort of it all; an unearthly echoing sound sending a shiver down Dominic's spine as he clicked the safety on the Glock and levelled it, pointing directly at Dickson.

"If you think you are going to knock my brains out with that bloody rock, the state you are in, tells me you may need a little assistance."

Dominic smiled as he delivered the words.

"Oh no, my little Spanish friend, I have something much more interesting in mind for you...!"

With that, Dickson summoned every last ounce of his remaining energy and launched the rock, not aiming directly at Dominic, but a few feet to his left side. Alvarez let loose a round from the pistol, hitting Dickson squarely in the chest and he fell to the ground. The rock, thrown by Dickson, moved several feet through the air and then dropped to Dominic's left, rolling downhill in the direction of the cave entrance.

Dominic watched, fascinated as the rock gathered momentum. Finally, it collided with a much bigger specimen on the edge of the opening. He had become completely transfixed by the event until the realisation struck him. The rock toppled over the edge taking an area of supporting ground with it about fifteen to twenty feet in all directions, including the section required to support the weight of Dominic Alvarez. He immediately disappeared into the blackness of the cave ... without a single sound.

Dickson lay on the ground, pain-free but bleeding profusely, knowing he had little time left, his final words shouted as loud as his retreating energy would allow.

"Nineteen ... unlucky for some ... and certainly unlucky for you, my friend!"

William (Billie) Dickson, military hardman and Special Forces operative was no more. Dominic Alvarez, vengeance seeking entrepreneur, died instantly from a massive bleeding wound to the head caused by primary impact with the floor of the cave. The two bodies would not be discovered for several months after the event ... with both deaths pronounced as 'unlawful'.

THE END

The Prisoner
Angela Dunn

He looked around the steel box that was to be his new home. Home for however long …? It would not do for him to dwell on it. That was at the mercy of others, out of his control ... the story of the wretched existence that was his life. Home, he mused, not a home. A holding cell for him to wait for his time to come. For his death, he supposed; the final long rest.

"Stick to what you can control," he whispered to himself firmly. "Don't let the monsters wear you down."

He wasn't sure which monster he was referring to. His world was full of monsters; he was a monster himself.

The click of the lock echoed in the remaining silence; a final punctuation point to end his relative freedom. 'But freedom from what?' he mused: the loneliness, the whispers, the pitying looks? The abject intolerance he faced from society because of his social status, or the fear that the rage would come again and this time he could not be stopped?

If that was freedom, he did not want it. At least here he was safe; the only person he could hurt now was himself. Society was safe too, at least from him. They could go to their warm beds and their three-course meals knowing that another poor person was not their problem.

He sighed. He had known it would end this way.

He was relieved it had ended this way. Now he was fed and had a bed. The only struggle was against himself, and he could handle that. He knew, in reality, he couldn't, but that was now the problem of others. His desperate act had made it that way; made people take notice now, way too late. When one didn't have money, one did not matter to those in power. The lack of health insurance had meant his health got worse, and the voices and urges became stronger.

The harsh fluorescent lights showed off his new surroundings. A metal shelf that served as a bed, screwed into the wall as standard; a thin, lumpy mattress that had seen better days; a desk and chair of sorts; a toilet and sink combination for hygiene, and a space where he could just about pace and stretch his legs.

"Luxury," he muttered sarcastically as he sat down on the bed. The bright orange of his prison uniform caught his eye; a bit of colour to break up the dull metallic grey. He tried to make himself comfortable on the mattress and smiled to himself. He deserved this, but it was worth it. He would do it all over again given the circumstances. He reflected that he had not wanted to do it in the first place. Maria would be sad. Maria was gone. Everyone was gone. The isolation of the cell was now just a physical manifestation of what his mind already faced. It was somewhat comforting to the prisoner in a way. His body and mind were in harmony, for the first time in as far back as he could remember.

He had already admitted his guilt and pled guilty at the first chance, so sparing another family the agony of a long, drawn-out trial. He had wanted the world, (or at least those that would care,) to know what he had done. He had wanted them to know why, wanted everyone to have his true love's name on their lips, their topic of conversation for a change to come. That was his hope - that someone would now take notice of his community and the plight they faced.

When the justice system let him down, he had no choice; he had to take things into his own, forever sin-stained hands. Maria deserved justice. He had delivered it. It was as simple as that. He had at least shown mercy compared to what Maria had suffered. Did not want to stoop to the level Maria's killer had done. Clean, efficient, job done! One more cancer cut away from the fabric of life. He had at least let the rich man's family say goodbye, which felt important to the prisoner.

They wouldn't let him see her body. He didn't get to say goodbye to his love. They said it would be too traumatic. He could understand that. Once upon a time he had wanted to be a police officer, to try to put some justice into the world in the right way. Nothing fancy like a detective; he had no illusions he was smart enough to make it that far. A uniformed officer, a face his community could relate to. But he had failed the exams, his brain unable to grasp the complex rules and regulations such a job required.

They buried what they had been able to find of his wife. DNA had been used to identify her scattered remains. Her killer's DNA was found in her hair, her fingertips, and her mouth. She had not gone down without a fight. She gave the police the best chance she could to identify her killer.

Yet, they messed it up despite that. Her killer was sent to freedom on a technicality. The prisoner was certain he would never understand the ins and outs, but he did understand her killer was free. An older, rich, powerful, and corrupt man so of course he was not going to face just punishment. He understood that well enough, had seen it endless times before. Money could make anything go away. Money could silence witnesses and bribe a judge. Money meant the law wouldn't apply. The prisoner felt sick at the thought of it.

He also understood that Maria was never coming back home. He would never feel the touch of her embrace. He would never hear her laugh or see the way her dimples appeared in her cheeks when she smiled. The scent that was unique to her was gone forever. The taste of her cooking, the joy she had when she sang. That was her favourite thing in the world to do, sing. She was always singing be it at church or simply while cleaning the dishes. All wiped out in a calculated and callous fashion.

People would say she should have known her place and kept her mouth shut. Others said she was asking for it and had tempted him with her womanly shape. She should have expected it. That it was just the boss being the boss. You just got on with it and he would reward you big. An open secret nobody would admit to.

But people were wrong. Her only crime had been to say no. Her only mistake was to think HR could be trusted. She should have been safe from her creep of a boss. This should have been a new start, a way out of the poverty trap society seemed determined to keep them in. She had finally made her way up in the world, a receptionist in some swanky office block. Better than the work she had in the supermarket as a checkout girl.

She had been so excited when she got the job offer. She had treated the pair to some actual real fresh chicken. It was so much better than the canned mystery meat from the food bank. And he, he had just been accepted into community college. It wasn't much, but it was something, a step in the right direction.

But her boss was not used to hearing the word no, not used to women speaking up for themselves. Surrounding himself with bootlickers and yes men, Maria was the first to reject him. The boss acted to make sure she was the last.

So, the prisoner himself had acted. He had tried to move on at first. He had choked down the serotonin and the sertraline; he had done the therapies: and turned to religion. He drank the alcohol; attended the support groups. All the stuff that was supposed to help him, didn't. The services were not in place to keep him stable, safe, and sane.

A rage burned inside of him. Like an itch that had to be scratched, consuming his days until he was just vengeance and revenge. There was only one way to make it stop. Only one cure for his ills. Do what had to be done. That was all he had left, the only purpose his life now held. The only clear voice that his fragile mind could comprehend. The devil, not an angel. Maria had been the angel that rescued him and made him want to be better, to get better, and do better. But Maria was gone. The only one who cared, snatched away on a rich man's say so.

So he had given in to the voice. Given himself the much-needed cure; did the deed and taken the life of the monster that had killed his Maria.

He couldn't remember how. Not exactly. He could piece certain parts together but not the full details. It was quick and clean. The lack of blood spatter testified to that. And it was personal; he remembered seeing the life leave his victim's face; the panicked look in his eyes as he gasped for air that wouldn't come. The prisoner thought for a moment: ah! That was right, he had used his fists, his height advantage, and his muscle to get the task done. At that point, he still couldn't tell if he was trying to kill Maria's murderer, the devil in his head, or both.

He felt oddly calm, focused. He thought he should have felt anger, grief, something? But it was as routine as pouring himself a bowl of cornflakes. And afterward came a rush of relief, as the boss's security dragged him away, stopping him from going any further. He had not hurt anyone innocent and that was the main point.

It didn't matter, the job was done. Purpose fulfilled; the need for vengeance satisfied. The voice finally silenced despite his screaming for help. Both man and devil despatched at the same time. It was good.

Finally, he felt at peace.

Inside the cell, the man smiled at the thought. Peace. It was ironic to him. An act of monstrous violence had finally allowed him to move on. Let him just be and breathe properly. The voice silenced at last.

As he sat on the poor excuse for a bed, he made a vow. He would bear the isolation as that was his punishment. A voice deep inside of him knew that it was for the best. He was alone now to mourn Maria and society was safe from his rage.

He knew once all the arguments were done, there was only one way his life would be allowed to end; a cycle of vengeance would start again, this time when the state had flicked the switch. He shrugged at the thought, it didn't scare him.

Nothing scared him as much as his mind terrified him. Except, maybe, that scream from along the corridor. The sound echoed from cell to cell, of grief, of pain, of rage, and of despair. It was a sound he had heard before, had made himself. The scream of someone who was now lost. The sound of madness personified. Another victim fallen to the devil as isolation and emotional toil got to them.

He heard the familiar crash as bone met metal, once, twice, three times; the sound of the guard's footsteps, rushing to restrain the poor soul. Maybe they would drug him, maybe they wouldn't. It briefly brought back a deeply buried memory from the sound of the streets he grew up in.

Another mother wailed as her son was lost.

Another child's life ended by a gang member's gun!

The prisoner dismissed it and gave the security camera in the corner of his cell a wave. Showers would be off the agenda tonight as the guards locked the area down even tighter. The scream stopped.

No doubt he would get used to the sounds and daily rhythms of the area he was held in. He couldn't help himself, not really. He certainly couldn't help anyone else.

He picked out his bible from the bundle of things the prison had issued him and began to read. The familiar words were both strange and comforting to him. It was something he had left, a connection to his wife. That was their thing, church on a Sunday without fail. Silence fell once more.

He smiled as he read. He knew that someday he would be reunited with his Maria, in the next life; alone no more.

THE END

The Target
T.H.

There is a man sitting at the café table … let's call him Mark. This is not his real name of course, but he has adopted so many names for his professional purposes, what's just one more? Mark, then, is congratulating himself on having found the perfect point from where to observe his object of interest. The decorative columns of the café are inlaid with mirrored surfaces. By inclining his upper body to the right Mark is able to keep watch on a table three places behind him, and yet remain unseen.

The woman, from Mark's view, is simply a head of close-cropped brown hair and a white top. The head frequently shakes in disagreement. Her partner talks earnestly between sips from his cup.

'Oh, oh, a lovers' quarrel', thinks Mark, shifting slightly in his chair to ease the pressure of the holstered pistol tucked below his left armpit. Around him plates clatter, cutlery scrapes and clicks, the coffee machine gurgles and shushes. Across the aisle, parents persuade a reluctant child to finish his chips. A young woman, carrying a baby, pushes a buggy, threading her way between the tables.

A wheel judders against Mark's table, an apologetic smile as she disengages the buggy and continues on her way. From the toilets, set at the far end of the café, a man emerges, led by a harnessed dog. It navigates its owner's way safely along the narrows of the aisle and as it passes Mark's table the dog turns its head, giving a brief wag of the tail.

For a second, Mark is looking into soft brown eyes, hearing a boy's voice calling the name 'Bob! Bob!' Yes, he reflected; the mongrel, born on a farm and condemned to the farmer's shotgun.

'It'll do nowt but eat and sleep.'

Ambushed by the memory, Mark drags his eyes back to the mirror. Damn!

His quarry is already on the move, heading through the plate-glass doors out onto the walkway beyond. Mark watched him turn left which means he will walk down the stairs to the lower level out onto the street; then, either a left or a right turn.

Mark has done his homework, of course. Which direction the man takes will determine his tactics. Now, count to five, nothing hurried; nothing obvious.

He moves past the table where the woman, now in profile to Mark, gazes after her man with a concerned look.

Mark, standing at the top of the stairs, glimpses his prey turning right, heading into the now derelict old town centre. What business could he possibly have there; a private meeting perhaps?

A complication, but easily solved.

This is the part of the process a professional enjoys: follow, but not be seen to follow, tracking intently, but appearing to be on a purposeless stroll. It calls on all his skills.

By now the glass fronted shops have given way to shuttered premises or boarded-up windows and entrances showing early signs of neglect and decay.

Two or three turns later, he heads into the dead heart of the district, a world of smashed glass, grey half-bricks and piles of rubble.

From a distance, a sudden muted roar is carried toward him by the wind. It's three o'clock. He once more feels strong arms lift him up, his face brushing past the heavy woollen scarf. Now, he is taller than all the crowds of big men around them and looking down from his perch on his dad's shoulders into a big field of grass …

Focus!

"Keep your attention on the job in hand!"

Mark looks around him. Some jagged half-walls with worn doorsteps still locked in place, leading to single courses of bricks outlining the rooms of vanished buildings, like a blueprint laid in the grass. The sight so familiar: just two up, two down and one room kept for best; cellars now gaping open to the sky; one or two houses remaining, bare-raftered and surviving only as shells.

Without doubt, a perfect killing ground in his expert opinion. A faded board, half-hidden in the grass and rubble displayed 'Last Chance Salo' in faint grey lettering and the half-wall above proclaims 'MAD LADZ ROOL' in red letters illustrated by a crude logo.

A single bullet …

One bullet is always sufficient in Mark's view. He switches his gaze to look down the road, the broken road flanked by cracked paving, half-flags and gaps in bare earth. For a moment he feels the pressure of the crowd bearing him along the narrow pavement, full of pushing, jostling shoppers. He is carried helplessly on the surge, trying to keep sight of his mother's green coat ahead.

He fights off the memory.

'Never go back!'

A quick scan across the area of broken desolation confirms few places of cover. His prey must have turned into one of the few remaining side openings, a kind of half-walled backstreet.

A cautious glance round the corner and Mark is looking into a cul-de-sac. His victim is standing, facing the far end wall which is half-covered with cracked plaster and pitted with holes, resembling a wall left by the death squads after they complete their work; everything so familiar; only the sack-like slumped bodies missing.

Suddenly a voice breaks into Mark's thoughts,

"You are very good at …what you do. You must be expensive."

The voice is cool, well-modulated, echoing off the walls. The man turns. Mark's question holds a note of caution, doubt, growing realisation.

"How long?"

"Since the café, no, don't blame yourself … nothing you did."

Some form of signal then Mark ponders.

The family at the opposite table … too busy!

The girl and the baby buggy … a genuine accident?

"Of course, the blind man!"

"Unfortunately for him; blind from birth, but you are getting warmer. We humans have such limited senses. Dogs, however, so sensitive, hear beyond our range, noses that can pick up the faintest trace of a smell, even detect cancer."

"Thanks for the biology lesson, but your point is?"

"As a true professional you take great care of the tools of your trade. A dog now, so versatile, it can be trained to respond to, for example, the scent of gun-oil?"

"I could still carry out my mission, here … now!"

The intended victim looks beyond Mark's shoulder.

In that same confident tone says,

"Well timed, gentlemen,"

Then to Mark, "I think your mission has just been terminated."

Mark is aware of the crunch of feet on the shards of glass and brick chippings and two figures standing behind him, just outside of his line of sight.

The man continues,

"You still have a purpose, a job to complete, for me. My business rivals are ruthless people; I am forced to be equally so. If I let you go, shake hands and part the best of friends, they would simply hire another killer with ice for blood. Your dead body will send the message that they might understand. You are simply, what they call, collateral damage!"

Mark's target walks forward, dropping his eyes as he passes his victim, a nod of the head to the men standing behind.

The last sensation Mark feels is the cold

muzzle of the silencer pressed against the back of his skull. The last sound, the 'phut' of the bullet leaving the barrel and his last thought; perhaps some level of admiration for the professionalism of his killers, a thought finally shredded by the bullet tearing through the cortex of his brain.

Mark ... yes, perhaps it was a very appropriate name after all.

THE END

Trials and Tribulation
Christine Turnbull

A wakening from a restless sleep, delegating those dreams to the plethora of past dreams which are dotted in the space assigned for things 'not real'. So real is the feeling of hunger, never feeling full or satisfied, eagerly awaiting the next offering of food, resigned to having to wonder, to imagine, to salivate with thoughts of food yet to be eaten.

Stirring, stretching and looking round the bright colourful room, taking in its scenes of playful characters. Superheroes galore, fighting battles which are always won, maybe by the baddies, in order to fire up the imagination even more.

There is a knocking and pounding against the window pane; the outside world, with its heavy downpour of rain, seemingly ever present. Gone are the white, soft, glistening snow crystals which covered the trees, manifesting into ghosts in the distance. Remembering the crunch when attempting to run, falling to the ground with its puddles, penetrating, freezing dampness sneaking into plump, translucent fingers and toes until slithering back into the warmth becomes paramount.

Tasks for today have been set since yesterday; those too having been assigned to 'things not real' now needing to be dragged to the fore. Treads can be heard coming closer, bright, light joyful steps ...

nearly there; a loud echoing tuneless song to wake up the sleepiest from their slumbers.

Quickly! Needing to prepare for the battle ... chose a sword, a shield and a gun; items needed to ambush the unsuspecting foe, with each turn of the handle, wait and watch then a slash of the sword, squeeze of a trigger as the monster crosses the threshold into the kingdom of dragons. Down goes the monster to the floor in the gentlest of ways, eyes closed very still and silent. Jumping up and down with glee, the monster is slain, battle won. It's time now to wake up the monster, with a kiss and tight cuddle.

The real world momentarily interrupts the fantasy, a bath with blue bubbly water, pirates raiding ships, with captors seized then forced to walk the plank. Then a whirlwind picks up the swirling blue sea sending it down; down into the dark never-ending hole.

The pirate, now on dry land, basks in the warmth of white fluffy clouds.

The day has passed without major transgressions. Concentration was needed and enforced, at least for a time, while objectives were achieved.

This evening excitement rises with thoughts of fun yet to be encountered. Enhanced are thoughts of simple delights; laughing, maybe some high fives, maybe a well done, rows of boys, all knowing the games to be played, the activities to be undertaken. The confusion, the roar of boys shouting run, run, pick it up, run then build it up, run back. The stern looks of some who want to win and occasionally praise for simply trying hard; a glow of joy is felt.

The games go on too long, concentration fades and eyes wander. Hands find alternate interests. Questions need answers; what is in this cupboard? What is behind this screen? Is it a desert island? Whose is this drink? I will just try it: running around looking for opportunities to entertain mind and body, blocking out all others.

Changing of the game, running, shoving to get away from the ball, to be given it then having the power to throw it at whoever passes by, standing waving arms wanting to catch; then, boys running again, dodging around in many directions. Energy now spent sitting on the bench, thoughts wondering onto many different plains finding one that fits the narrative currently playing in the 'not real' place.

Zombies have risen from the dark, wet earth, hungry, wild, hunting for delicious, slimy brains to eat. Stop the game and shout to all "run to safety!"

Best time to come. The lady has arrived. Time to focus, going into the previously forbidden cupboard passing out boxes of sweets and candies and drinks, the table filling up with treats, behind the table, standing tall, allowed to help serve the boys with chosen treats.

Warmth, envelopes, silence reigns, dreams come, occasional disturbances when dreams become vivid, encroaching into reality, when legs kick and thrashing occurs.

Today the monster is not so easily fought off, so simple a task to be survived becomes a mammoth mountain to ascend. Climbing up the mountain is obstructed by the clip, clip of scissors so sharp the frightening thoughts of skin being cut, the blood to run and the pain inflicted and maybe a head detached and rolling away. No, this mountain is too high to climb. Yet the snipping goes on, crying, shouting, pleading does no good, held tight not able to move; tears running as rivers. At last the top of the mountain is near; all is silent except for the sobbing.

Coming down from the mountain to a selection of treats, which one shall be mine? To relegate this memory to those 'not real' is survival for another day ... until the next time.

Entering into a known space, I look at the faces seated around tables, all smiling and chatting, welcoming to all. Time for giving and receiving cuddles so warm and sincere. Entering a space to explore jumping, running, climbing, watching as a large thick snake appears; people holding each end, a red flag in the middle, come, come and join in, clutch the snake one-two-three pull! To and fro the snake goes until the other side let go and fall laughing to the floor. A cheer goes up. Let's do it again, on and on until the snake is eventually lying exhausted on the floor.

Hoops roll, figures chasing, diving through to land in a heap, encouraged to try, feeling included, happy warm sensations rise within. Chatting people, with glasses in hand, ready for some fun, see who will be part of the games. Squeezing cuddles, gentle encouragement given and received, overjoyed as the participants laughingly do as they are bid, lifting weights, star jumps and squats are enjoyed under direction of course, do it right or not at all!

All now jolly, easy to mould, see what fun can be had with the smallest but strongest by far and two willing volunteers to lift the bar; congratulations, laughing voices shouting 'well done' fill the air.

Entertaining the adults is so easy, they laugh, they cheer; they say 'so cute.' If only the children could understand my ways. My imagination rules my thoughts, the games always floating in my mind, not easily transferred to others of similar age; to understand my actions, to enjoy my games and not to take affront at my touching and cuddling. It is part of me; a part easily rebuffed by children who are not able to give themselves to understand and accept my ways.

Perhaps as I grow the power of imagination will lessen, the need to cuddle will go ... and maybe they will know me.

THE END

AUTHOR BIOGRAPHIES

Chris Robinson

Chris Robinson was born in Hartlepool, and worked in London, briefly in banking, and then in an antiquarian booksellers.

He continued in general bookselling in Durham and Hartlepool, and then as an English language teacher in London, Middlesbrough and the Middle East before retiring back in Hartlepool.

.

Quentin Cope.
MA, MSc.

Surviving the uncomfortable consequences of Middle East conflict in the eighties and nineties, author Quentin Cope finally completed his Masters in Applied Arts/Science during 1995, having enjoyed a life of real adventure; some of it remembered as wonderfully exhilarating ... and some of it not!

As a diligent writer, Quentin's award-winning style can sometimes be seen as punchy, and often quite direct, revealing similar approaches to storytelling as Jack Higgins and Glover Wright. With more than thirty-four books in print, Quentin is a prolific and experienced wordsmith. His books sell worldwide on all Amazon platforms and online through major international book outlets.

T.H.

T.H. was born, brought up, lived and worked in the 'Hartlepools' for most of his life. After semi-retirement from teaching he spends his time struggling with the frustrations of water colour painting alongside the problems of researching local history and the perplexities of 'creative' writing.

Irene Styles

Irene Styles is a retired schoolteacher, born and bred in the North East of England. She recently emigrated with her husband to join her family in Canada and is kept busy with her grandchildren on beautiful Bowen Island.

Her new and idyllic surroundings provide inspiration for writing both poetry and short stories. Irene has had several pieces of her work published in anthologies and is one of our overseas members.

Mikaella Lock
BSc, MSc(R), MRSB

After a career working in biotech (venoms) and publishing in academic circles, Mikaella has always wanted to try her hand at writing creatively. She has a penchant for the macabre, the morbid, and the unusual.

An avid horror fan, Mikaella particularly enjoys writing shocking stories and tales of a darker nature. She also has a deep love of the natural world so when she's not penning stories about killers and psychopaths, she can be found happily painting, designing, and creating pretty things at her home studio.

T. R. Moran

Terry has been 'into' writing since he was ten years old. His favourite genre is horror, but we all love a good mystery now and then, don't we?

John Blackbird

John Blackbird is a writer who is from and lives in the seaside town of Hartlepool. He discovered writing in his late teens, after developing an increasing love for storytelling. He loves short stories, a good horror or action film and video games.

Ange Dunn

Ange Dunn is a hobby writer who wields a laptop mightier than any sword. With a diploma in Creative Writing and Literature from the Open University, they originally hailed from Hartlepool and moved on to Darlington where they now share a cosy apartment with their partner, Dave.

When not writing, Ange can be found baking tasty treats, playing Dungeons and Dragons, or indulging in musical theatre. A true geek at heart, they are passionate about politics, the custodian of a growing tea collection, and provider of a regular stop-off point for various animals, despite having no pets of their own. Ange's journey into writing began as a child, finding joy in storytelling thanks to the encouragement of their primary school teacher, Mr. Wise. Despite the challenges of dyslexia, Ange has embraced writing in all its forms, drawing inspiration from the MCU, Dan Smith, Robert Rankin, and more.

Ange's work has been published in the Hartlepool Writers Collection Anthology 2020. As a former NaNoWriMo ML for the Darlington and Tees region from 2019 to 2023, Ange has inspired many writers to embark on their literary adventures.

Christine Turnbull

Christine in her distant past was an army chef, now a retired nurse practitioner who fills her days with hiking, cycling, cross-fit, and an energetic ten year-old grandson.

Christine's passions include the outdoors, adventure, travelling, creative's, and hobbies such as knitting. She also loves a good crime book. To add another string to her already full bow writing has become her latest task even though she is dyslexic, so finds the written word challenging.

Robert Blackthorne

Robert Blackthorne is a proud resident of Hartlepool, born and raised. Since he was little, he always believed in the power of storytelling, helping us to understand the sometimes confusing world surrounding us.

Now, he hopes to share that same love of tall tales and modern-day fables with others, much like his Grandmother did before him. He hopes that readers will enjoy this series of collective works, and that just a few chosen words, perhaps hidden within these pages, may well inspire the reader to pursue a renewed interest in writing and the arts.

Colin Dunn

Being a fan of the 'beautiful game' alongside a passion for writing, Colin is a regular contributor to HWG group activities. He also spends time surrounding himself with books as a volunteer in his local libraries. For those of you who hold a particular interest in the game of 'soccer' or 'football' as some would prefer it ... The Red Card awaits!

THE END

Hartlepool Writers Group
2024

Web: www.hartlepoolwriters.co.uk
Email: hartlepoolwriters@gmx.com

Printed in Great Britain
by Amazon